Praise for *Woodwind Harmony in the Nighttime*

"Language, philosophers tell us, is not merely a tool of our thoughts and emotions but their organic component. Philosophers also tell us that exiles are custodians of 'dead treasures' and losing one's language is an often-inevitable part of the agonies of exile. Reza Ghassemi offers at once both a description of the pains of the Iranian exilic experience and a path for soothing, if not transcending it. He is an artist of myriad talents. A master tar player, a consummate composer, an innovative novelist whose passion for innovation equals his immersion in the traditions of Iranian and global modernities. In a dazzling text of rich allusions, almost rhythmic pace, and acute observations he masterfully describes the agonies of exile and the redemptive power of literature in describing our common humanity." —Abbas Milani, author of *The Shah*

"A fantastical and many-layered roller-coaster of displacement and redemption, funny and haunting by turns, with a thrilling edge of subversiveness. I enjoyed every bit of the ride, attempting along with the narrator to solve the mystery of exactly what has happened, and is happening, and why. Applause to translator Michelle Quay for her careful and delightful rendering, which retains all the sparkling wit and musicality for which Persian storytelling is known." —Tina Kover, translator of *Disoriental*

"Sometimes exile means trading the big, cruel world for a smaller universe of the sad and desperate stranded on the top floor of an aging Parisian apartment building. Reza Ghassemi's decidedly unharmonious Persian-Parisian symphony ricochets through its impossible but profoundly believable movements in Michelle Quay's utterly convincing translation."

—Shelley Fairweather-Vega, translator of *We Computers*

Woodwind Harmony in the Nighttime

Reza Ghassemi

Translated from the Persian by Michelle Quay

DEEP VELLUM PUBLISHING
DALLAS, TEXAS

Deep Vellum Publishing
3000 Commerce Street, Dallas, Texas 75226
deepvellum.org · @deepvellum

Deep Vellum is a 501c3 nonprofit literary arts organization founded in 2013 with the mission to bring the world into conversation through literature.

Originally published in Persian as همنوایی شبانه‌ی ارکستر چوب‌ها (*ham-navāi-ye shabāne-ye orkestr-e chub-hā*) by Nashr-e Ketab Corp., Los Angeles, CA, 1996

First English edition, 2026

Support for this publication has been provided in part by grants from the Texas Commission on the Arts, the City of Dallas Office of Arts and Culture, and the Addy Foundation.

LIBRARY OF CONGRESS CATALOGING-IN-PUBLICATION DATA

Names: Qāsimī, Riẕā author | Quay, Michelle translator
Title: Woodwind harmony in the nighttime / Reza Ghassemi ; translated from the Persian by Michelle Quay.
Other titles: Hamnavāyī-i shabānah-yi urkistr-i chūbhā. English
Description: First edition. | Dallas, Texas : Deep Vellum Publishing, 2025.
Identifiers: LCCN 2025034306 (print) | LCCN 2025034307 (ebook) | ISBN 9781646054190 trade paperback | ISBN 9781646054206 ebook
Subjects: LCGFT: Thrillers (Fiction) | Black humor | Novels | Fiction
Classification: LCC PK6561.Q29 H3613 2025 (print) | LCC PK6561.Q29 (ebook)
LC record available at https://lccn.loc.gov/2025034306
LC ebook record available at https://lccn.loc.gov/2025034307

Cover art and design by Elisha Zepeda
Interior layout and typesetting by KGT

PRINTED IN THE UNITED STATES OF AMERICA

Table of Contents

Like a Horse, but Not a Horse

It's not unusual for exiles to be paranoid It's not unusual for exiles to be paranoid It's not unusual for exiles to be paranoid . . . These words looped in my brain, for days and then weeks and then months, while I was rereading and rereading what's brought us here together: Reza Ghassemi's *Woodwind Harmony in Nighttime.* "It's not unusual for exiles to be paranoid" is by no means the most extraordinary sentence in this great classic of the Iranian postmodernist canon, full of extraordinary everythings, but the sentence just didn't want to let me go. ("I've become Ghassemified," I told a friend, who wondered what was wrong with me, and who of course had no idea what I meant by that.) The narrator of *Woodwind Harmony in Nighttime* announces "It's not unusual for exiles to be paranoid" to a boarding house full of exiled immigrants, and he's addressing us—some of us exiled immigrants ourselves—and he's addressing *me,* a writer and paranoid exile myself—who has been tasked with introducing this impossible book to you . . .

There is an ancient Chinese proverb that goes, "It's better to be a dog in a peaceful time than a man in a chaotic period," but what if we are all just dogs in a chaotic period? This is Ghassemi in a nutshell, but we'll get back to dogs and chaos in a moment.

Picture a dismal summer weekday. You, a middle-aged immigrant, are sitting in your nineteenth apartment rental in your adopted country—you have been a citizen exactly half your life—and you are deep in your writing and editing while also preparing some Persian comfort food with the news blaring in the background. Except it's not your news, but the neighbor's, an elderly Pakistani man, also an immigrant, who plays his CNN loudly, 24/7. Downstairs there is a Caribbean immigrant and upstairs an Eastern European immigrant, all of you cramped in a brownstone whose old glory you can sense, though that's been long muted by its current legacy of vermin, draftiness, fixtures in desperate wont of repair, and an absent super who hates you all for no real reason. (*It's not unusual for exiles to be paranoid.*) Somewhere tucked deep in New York's illustrious past, your abode was built for a family of one, opulent and spacious in a way this run-down, six-unit apartment building is not. You have no idea how the other residents feel because we're in an era where it's too harrowing to say anything, much less a normal *hello how are you* to any neighbor, but you do wonder how the old man can handle this 24/7 news, and how he regards the personal bits that always seem to catch your ear: the President's anti-immigrant rhetoric is what you tend to hear most loudly blaring. Did he turn the volume up, worried it applies to him, maybe even to all of us? It's as if there is no other consistent theme in the news but this news: POTUS wants immigrants out. (Out probably means dead, but at least out!) Although: *It's not unusual for exiles to be paranoid.* But. You get back to work and try to do this very work, and read as many Persian articles as you can on this book's author, searching for a clue on how to crack this book for its readers—have I called it *impossible* yet?—when you stumble over and over on your own name on its cover: "With an introduction by Porochista Khakpour" as if the thing exists, as if it has a life outside of you. This wouldn't be such a big deal—many publishers announce their books and their translators and intro writers well in advance of publication—if it didn't feel like an episode from the Ghassemi-verse, which in fact is a novel that ruthlessly interrogates itself as a novel. And here I am, the writer of the intro now a part of the novel's narrative, this introduction somehow having a life outside of me. I look at my name on the cover as the deadline approaches and passes. I wish I could say it's unusual for me to watch a deadline go by. What is less unusual: anti-immigrant rhetoric blaring incessantly as I work on a book about immigrant panic. On the news, filtered through the walls of my neighbor, the voice of the highest-ranking official of our adopted country: "animals," "stone-cold killers," "the worst people," "enemy from within," "poisoning the blood." *It's not unusual for exiles to be paranoid,* I hear. And of course, this is all done with my dog at my feet—which, well, wait until I explain the dog part . . .

•

Woodwind Harmony in the Nighttime is the debut novel of the great Iranian novelist, dramatist, and musician Reza Ghassemi, originally published in Persian in 1996 and masterfully translated here into English by Michelle Quay. Ghassemi himself emigrated from a war-torn Iran to France in 1986, and his life has been split among all kinds of arts—in fact, there are Iranians who know him as a classical sitar player and playwright as much as a novelist. But it's safe to say this very book is what has made him known most as a luminary of Iranian letters, particularly in the universe of contemporary Iranian fiction. It's received everything from the Golshiri Literary Award for Best First Novel in 2002 to more recently the Mo Habib Prize for Translation in 2023.

•

The story is misleadingly simple: an Iranian exile lives in a rented attic of a Paris boarding house in the 1990s, with a bunch of other immigrants, and chaos ensues. There are angels—or are there? It's also possible that at least on one narrative plane, our narrator isn't even alive! But one thing we know for sure is an awful sense of impending doom—pretty much on every page—compounded by both personal and collective turmoil: delusions, catastrophic thinking, superstitions, and hallucinations. Our narrator not only does nothing to establish his own reliability or even make a case for it, but he also continuously calls it into question and even suggests that the book mentioned in the text is the book the reader is reading. Ghassemi adds this metafictional element like a juggler adding another knife to an already treacherous knife-juggling act, and it nearly mutilates the whole enterprise. Nearly. In a novel of flashbacks and multiple timelines, we can't even rely on time. In several chapters, the bells of Saint Paul's Cathedral chime in to remind us of the passage of time, but even they drop out. Ideally, you'll read this book several times despite the disorientation of the first read: the provocations, the frustrations, the exhaustion, the moments you want to throw the book down. You'll read and reread entire passages because they enthrall and/or baffle you.

•

In the beginning, there was Kafka—or rather, by the end of the book, there most certainly was. Who could resist thinking of Kafka's *Metamorphosis* when Ghassemi insists on a horse simile: "I was like a horse that had sensed impending disaster." But Ghassemi warms you up to the antics of his semantic hopscotch: "You've seen how their eyes bug out, right? How they snort the fear swirling around in their skulls out their trembling nostrils? How they whinny and stomp their hooves? No, I haven't seen it either. But if I were a horse, that's how I'd express my terror." Enter unreliable narrator as narrative underminer. Like a horse, but not a horse, but even this possibility/impossibility—here we go again, spoiler ahead—fulfills itself with the final bookend of our Kafkascape, where our narrator's final form is none other than a dog, and not just any dog, but the dreaded big black dog who belongs to the landlord. This is unadulterated, pure Kafka, but without panic and terror: resignation and even boredom might be the final surprising note of this slender novel, a canine's placid temperament placed against a backdrop of psychedelic delusion and illusion. But we're not even given much room to imagine any of this—are we really to buy our narrator is the constantly pissing-where-he-should-not-be, oft-mistreated, rarely-appreciated black dog Gabik? In fact, we're not even sure if Gabik is Gabik: the landlord's wife lets us know they've had several similar dogs replacing dead ones, successors to the original black dog Gabik. If only our narrative was as straightforward and simple as Kakfa's pact with Samsa; instead, we are misled by a conceptual horse and end up not just confronted but also inhabited by a version of a dog negotiated by angels.

For the nihilistic themes in his work, Kafka is a clear precursor to Ghassemi, but there are even more literary forefathers. Over the years, critics and theorists have invoked Kurt Vonnegut, John Barth, Milan Kundera, Vladimir Nabokov, Thomas Pynchon—all to say, it seems, that *Woodwind Harmony* is experimental, maximalist, dark, hilarious, and, to put it mildly, challenging. For me, another obvious influence hits close to home: Sadegh Hedayat's 1937 modernist masterpiece *The Blind Owl.* (Full disclosure: I wrote the intro to a popular Grove edition). In Hedayat's fever-dream thriller, an artist losing his sanity in a nightmarish self-imposed isolation reflects on his life in cycles of paranoia that ultimately form a kind of murder confessional. In *The Blind Owl,* our narrator tailors his own audience from a shadow on the wall that he decides resembles an owl; in *Woodwind Harmony,* the shadow is purely a double, like unwanted company, an audience you can never shake as much as you try. Whereas *The Blind Owl* is insular and claustrophobic in its examination of alienation, Ghassemi's novel is maddeningly social in its overpopulated, involuntary close quarters. Our narrator is in his cramped sixth-floor apartment, but we don't get a minute's rest from the apartment complex and all its inhabitants and their many intersecting dilemmas. Loneliness, while a theme, is not the real problem here—or at least not the loneliness we'd first imagine. Ghassemi goes beyond the melancholia of Hedayat's somber reclusion. Ghassemi proposes you don't have to be away from society to feel alone—you could be surrounded by a girlfriend and friends and neighbors and landlords and their pets even, and still feel a profound seclusion. In fact, one could argue that the polyphonic disorder that overwhelms Ghassemi's protagonist easily outdoes the horror of being a prisoner of one's own failing mind in Hedayat's version of hell.

In reality, both Hedayat and Ghassemi were immigrants living in a France that never quite became their home. A key distinction: Hedayat ultimately succumbed to suicide there, and Ghassemi to this day thankfully thrives. But as anti-immigrant rhetoric becomes increasingly normalized in far-right governments all over the world, the horrors of exile are unmistakable and emerge in shades of mania or depression. Aside from the obvious dangers, presumed allies infantilize the victims. These "friends" yearn for the adversity of the migration struggle to feel noble and to be moved. They need their hearts broken to believe in our cause. But what if immigrants themselves didn't see it that way—what if, after the experiment of exile, their conclusion was to avoid all that and return to their native land? Certainly the surreal nightmares of these Iranian authors could provide its own kind of fuel for those opposing immigration, if only those opponents were intelligent enough to untangle complex narratives.

•

Oddly enough, the most grounding element in *Woodwind Harmony at Nighttime* is what is often most nebulous in the Iranian canon: theme. When allegory and abstraction are at play, the foundation feels sturdiest. The novel is a parable of the shadow self. Ghassemi's narrator explains himself early on:

> How can I tell Bernard that a man in the desert always lives with his shadow? Everywhere he goes, his shadow is there with him, right or left. Everywhere he goes, he follows his shadow or drags it along behind him. He is only free from his shadow for one moment, just for a single moment: high noon. When the lances of the sun's rays strike the crown of the head.

Ghassemi knows that for someone in this kind of true solitude "the only possession of value is his shadow." The shadow is always there, even when you cannot perceive it. "When he sits, it sits with him. When he stands, it stands too. In the morning, it stretches its height to the western horizon. In the evening, it stretches to the east. What human is that loyal?" Therefore to triumph against the self, one has to go beyond the corporeal. The real object should be the shadow. "That these shots I fire into my own foot are really shots aimed at my shadow. A shadow that usurped me and has sat angrily in my place for years." By the penultimate chapter, Ghassemi poses the question: if the shadow is always the winner, does triumph exist if the struggle is its own zone of comfort? "The struggle between me and the shadow had been dragging on so long," Ghassemi writes, "when I was finally free of it, I'd become addicted to the struggle itself. The struggle became my reason for being, my life's meaning."

The predicament becomes especially interesting when you consider one of the central dilemmas of the book—and a dominant allegory—is our narrator's inability to see his own reflection, the inverse dilemma of the shadow. Ghassemi again explains with a charmingly banal matter-of-factness:

> The first time I became aware of this symptom, I acted like someone who'd just bought a VCR. I was sure the lack of a picture was a minor issue that could be resolved with a bit of tinkering, so I started experimenting with the mirror. Actually, once or twice I was able to get the reflection of the razor back for a second while I was messing around with it. Just like that, the razor was moving up and down all by itself, no hand or face in sight.

His conclusion is as simple as it is extraordinary: "My mirror only reflected inanimate objects." This becomes a concrete way for our narrator to register his own existence—to evaluate which body parts are more dead than others. In *Woodwind's* universe, the fact that the mirror only reflects the nonliving suggests that the living are mere ghosts. But we don't question it and, like our narrator, applaud the metric for its utility: "Anytime I doubted whether I was alive or not, I would go to the mirror and say to myself, 'See? It doesn't show your reflection. So you must not have turned into an inanimate object yet!'"

Why would the tyranny of the shadow and the unreflected self matter so much in a book like this? One reason is the self in question is a very transparently engineered self: the storyteller as a metafictional invention. In the world of a story, "author" is the most suspect vocation. It's never by accident when our narrator claims to be a writer. Not only has our narrator written a book, but also—like Hedayat's protagonist—he spends his missing hours painting in his room (a task that is sometimes at odds with the writing, curiously: "I said I was painting, but really, I was editing the book most nights.") Of course, the additional fun is that it brings the reader in as well: if the author is a character, then so is its partner, the receiving end of the ball's arc, the reader as the other half of the compact. Ghassemi lets us be co-conspirators to plot the very book we're reading: "You confirm that these notes belong to a book by the name of *Woodwind Harmony in the Nighttime*, which you published under a pseudonym?" "No, that's not true. The book was never published." "That's the same answer you gave in the book!" The realism in the comedy and the comedy in the realism, which every writer will find familiar—if not from actual experience then from their nightmares: "Every publisher I sent it to said bluntly, 'These ramblings are not literature and I've wasted my time.'" But we know the mirroring—a key word, of course!—of the novel as the book's subject, with the novel as the object we're reading, is yet another game of shadows. "I had written *Woodwind Harmony* years ago, way before all that stuff happened," the narrator tells us. "A totally made-up story. I didn't know any of the characters, in those days. Not even Seyyed or Ra'na. Then my life started to mirror the book." The tug of war between art and life yields surprising results. Our narrator realizes his power in a world that fears the power of art, but he also realizes his willingness to relinquish that power:

> I wanted to change the fate that awaited me by rewriting the plot (an effort that was sadly unsuccessful, since I very quickly realized I had to either ruin my book or ruin my life). Second, after Seyyed and Ra'na somehow caught wind I was writing the book, every time we saw each other they tried to figure out what I'd written, and at the same time, they tried to justify or twist the events of the past, so I would revise my judgment. Well, you know a writer should have some sympathy for his protagonists, so I watered things down or adjusted them a bit, especially because the way they acted put me in a most enjoyable position: I saw that their fear of literature was stronger than the fear of Judgment Day.

By Chapter Five ("Handknit Socks, Made in Iran"), even the landlord picks up the book, bookmarked with a tenant's unpaid rent notice, and opens to page 177, which is the page we the reader happen to be on as well. (In my Word doc version of the manuscript, I was delighted to find a note from translator Michelle Quay that highlighted "177" with a note: "This should match the page number in the actual printed book.")

Of course there is something fitting about these literary pyrotechnics in a novel where the unreliability of the narrator is emphasized from the first page. There is no baseline sanity here and normalcy is always up for debate. In a way, it seems clear that Ghassemi is not talking about some invented world, but asking that we very honestly face the true nature of ours:

> For a moment, I felt that I had gone mad. But how can an insane person distinguish the line between madness and sanity? Anyone whose mental stability has been destroyed starts out on a path, and it ends in a place called insanity. But where is this place? Without a doubt, some people stop after advancing some ways down the path and, if circumstances allow, turn around and slowly go back the way they came. This place, however—this border between lucidity and lunacy, which is invisible until we've crossed it—would we be aware of it if we had traversed it? Certainly, for others the question is clear. But what about for ourselves? Haven't you seen those crazy people who warn you they're not crazy and you, all of you onlookers, laugh at them? So is it possible that I too have crossed over this line and am unconscious of it?

But there's a range of disorder for the reader of this novel to take in. On the one hand, when our narrator says, "It's not unusual for exiles to be paranoid," we can all basically agree. On the other hand, when we read, "So was it possible I'd killed someone and didn't know it?"—a line has been crossed. So much of the novel's interior world—the interiority of our main character in the interior of the boarding house, an insular world that could be anywhere—feels cracked, and yet through the cracks another world comes in. Has our narrator gone too far? Has he lost us? Is his story going to catch up with him?

We don't need to worry because Ghassemi decides that fabulism will have the final word. Indeed, when our narrator becomes a dog, there is little left to reason with. Early in the book, the narrator hints at this curse when introducing Gabik:

> I wasn't afraid of the dog. Or at least, for a while now I hadn't been scared out of my mind when I saw him, or disgusted when I touched him. Of course, getting to this point wasn't easy. In the culture I grew up with, dogs were unclean creatures, and the slightest brush against one meant you were contaminated . . . Worse still, if people wanted to curse you, they'd turn you into a dog. There were people who had committed so many sins that they'd been reincarnated as a dog after their death.

We can only assume the contract is kept; our final paragraph catalogues the sins leading to the ultimate curse. Oddly, the tone doesn't change, which tells us more about our narrator than the dog. "I return to my spot and stretch out between the legs of the chairs. Tomorrow, I'm going to sleep easy. Tomorrow, when I piss in the hallway, Mathilde will forget. Tomorrow, Mathilde won't remember I did the same thing the day before. Every time she'll think it's the first time. Which is right now. 'Right now.'"

Ultimately, the absurdity connects to the identity loss, which takes us back to the issue of exile. Here is the restlessness of being Iranian, from a nation of constant conquest and endless displacement, what I called in my Hedayat intro "a country of homeland seekers with a destination only in their ancient past." Hedayat, like our narrator, "could not find solace in Tehran society and yet in Paris he could not find peace either. He was the Iranian nationalist who, fed up with the corruptions of church and state alike, was perpetually looking westward; he was also the foreigner in Europe, whose daily life was endless visa applications and intense economic hardship, whose eyes were cast to the comforts of his mother country where he was of the aristocracy." We could sense this from Ghassemi too.

I thought of this and how we often joke that Iranians always like to obscure their roots—sometimes going as far as claiming a connection to royalty—when I encountered this favorite passage:

> With this outlook, it was no wonder he introduced me, a simple house painter, as the greatest painter in the country, and himself as one of the residents of Qom, the name of an Iranian city which suddenly became 'Rome' when pronounced with a French accent. That's why, the day he changed his nationality, he gave himself the name 'Alexander.' Eventually, he even produced a family tree from his father's heirlooms that showed he was descended from Italian nobility.

Having written a last novel where my protagonist literally fakes being Italian for most her life to hide her more controversial Iranianness, I was taken aback by this recognition. The rest of the world's jokes about us have never been very effective; the best joke has always been on us *by us*. Perhaps this is why we're such masters of the darkest comedy, the most intense satires, the most harrowing parodies. Even with all the mentions of Pink Floyd, KFC, Faust, Gary Cooper, even *One Flew Over the Cuckoo's Nest, Woodwind Harmony* is as Eastern as Hedayat's *The Blind Owl*. An East that's found itself stuck in the West. An East that has become reluctantly Western. And most notably, that transformation is engineered by the West, who for decades has made a business of creating refugees in the Middle East. Not even the trickiest narrative labyrinth can obscure this reality. This central betrayal is at the core of every major work of Iranian migration literature.

At one point, the narrator describes acting in a play apparently directed by our author: "The director—a tyrannical, grouchy man called Ghassemi—sent me up on the stage under the glare of a bright light and said: 'Keep repeating that line until I tell you to stop.' For the first few minutes, I repeated the line the same way, but he never told me to stop." At first the narrator says the line the same way, over and over, then changes it up out of boredom, then ultimately breaks down, pleading, and finally gets exasperated, even threatening, before again resorting to pleas. It's all part of the director's vision: "This was his goal all along—to bring me to this point. I started the line again, and this time delivered it with gratitude, singing it in an exhilarated tone, 'Forgive me! Forgive me!'" This negotiation between actor and director, narrator and author, haunted me for weeks. It's hard to know what to do with this late episode of the novel, so close to the end—but in the context of Iranianness, it left me with a cold chill. If Ghassemi is playing the God of our universe, then it's up to us to break the pattern he's designed. We won't get that permission from him. The conundrum has to break us down first, most likely more than a few times. And in the end, when we approach the revelation that's supposed to liberate us, are we even really ready to receive it? Have we arrived? Or do we just want it all to stop? How much of the meaninglessness is by design and how much of it just *is*?

Reader, I don't know. I can't tell you. You'll have to decide for yourself. This paranoid exile tried to be the proverbial man in a peaceful time, but all I got was chaos and dog. Here we are. When you read this, my old immigrant neighbor, if alive, will still be blasting anti-immigrant sentiments on his television all day and all night, and we'll all be dreaming of a better day that likely won't come—maybe even waiting for the angels who can punish us for our sins. I wish I could end this on a more hopeful note. For now, we're on that stage, under the bright lights, and the director has not yet told us to stop. We're in the middle, somewhere between relentless frustration and flimsy gratitude. Only the tyrannical director knows how much longer before the curtain drops, the lights go out, and then, just maybe, it can all be over.

Porochista Khakpour
November 2025

Translator's Note

The year is 2001, and Iranian writers are enjoying unprecedented freedom from censorship under reformist president Mohammad Khatami. In the Ministry of Culture and Islamic Guidance, an editor walks up to Booth 26, hoping to get permission to publish a novel. This state apparatus ensures all published literature in the country meets religious (and political) standards. The body calls itself "The Distinguisher." The public knows it as "The Censor." The moment the editor tosses his novel on the counter, the censor glances at the title and says, "Oh, *Woodwind Harmony* . . ." He pushes it back across without missing a beat. "I've read this one. Go publish it." And the editor scurries on his way, with a soon-to-be literary phenomenon tucked under his arm.

In 2025, such a breezy experience at the censorship department is unthinkable. The brief window of freedom experienced by Iranian writers between 1998 and 2002 quickly slammed shut. In the years following the surge in the publication of uncensored books, many employees were purged from the Ministry or arbitrarily detained. Reza Ghassemi, the author of *Woodwind Harmony in the Nighttime*, says he later met his censor in exile in Paris and had the chance to thank him personally.

Censorship affects every form of media being produced in Iran today. It forces writers to alter their writing or use cryptic symbolism to circumvent government agencies who want to control their work. *Woodwind Harmony in the Nighttime*, however, stands in an unusual position. Because it was originally published in Los Angeles in 1996 and later republished during the Khatami era in Iran in 2002, it has been uninfluenced by censorship, widely read in the Persian-speaking diaspora, and acclaimed within Iran in its uncensored form. As a scholar of Persian literature, I was shocked to learn that Nilufar Press managed to acquire permission to publish this novel inside Iran without making any changes to the manuscript. Veiled political references aside, it contains a number of allusions to sex or drinking that would normally, by today's standards, never make it through to publication. The censors may also object to instances of "immoral" behavior, which this novel is full of. *Woodwind Harmony*, it seems, just happened to be in the right place at the right time.

One of the great joys of Ghassemi's text is the evident freedom he feels writing from his adopted home in Paris, far away from the meddling reach of the censors. Ghassemi's fresh new style and themes helped turn the novel into a literary hit upon publication. It inspired a BBC Persian documentary on his life and work, and garnered great acclaim amongst critics and readers alike. In 2002, it was awarded the Golshiri Prize for Best First Novel, which, at the time, was Iran's top literary honor. A few years later, it was voted Best Novel of the Decade by the Iranian Society of Critics and Writers. As such, it is unlike some contemporary works of Persian diaspora literature, which may be acclaimed in the West, but remain largely unknown inside Iran. (For example, Iranian exile Shokoofeh Azar's *Enlightenment of the Greengage Tree* was nominated for the

International Booker Prize in 2020, but the author has never had any of her work published in Iran.)

At its heart, Reza Ghassemi's novel is a story about the rupture of immigration. Specifically, it meditates on how living in exile shatters the immigrant's unified sense of self. Told in the first-person voice of Yadollah, who has recently immigrated to 1990s Paris, the very structure of the novel reflects its theme of fragmentation. The narrative bounces back and forth between Yadollah's life on the sixth floor of a run-down apartment building and his afterlife, where he is unceremoniously interrogated by the Islamic angels of death, Nakeer and Monkar. In this case, however, Nakeer and Monkar are humorously reimagined as Faust from F. W. Murnau's eponymous 1926 film, and Chief Bramson, the Native American patient from *One Flew Over the Cuckoo's Nest* (1975), respectively.

But it is not just the life/afterlife split in the narrative that contributes to the reader's sense that they are piecing together fragments when reading Ghassemi's work. Yadollah confesses very early on that he suffers from multiple self-diagnosed and mysterious diseases, most notably the time gap disease, which causes him to experience jumps in time and lapses in memory. He also believes his body has been occupied by a shadow since the traumatic death of his beloved at the age of fourteen. This shadow-possession means his reflection does not appear in the mirror, once again suggesting the theme of the fragmented self.

Though subtle, there are political undertones to the novel, which may be difficult for the non-Iranian reader to grasp. Ghassemi began writing the novel in 1990, in the aftermath of the Islamic Revolution of 1979, which dramatically swept Ayatollah Khomeini to power and led to the bloody Iran-Iraq War of 1980-1988. Following the revolution, the new Islamic Republic of Iran developed sophisticated intelligence networks to surveil, threaten, and eliminate political opponents both at home and abroad. Domestically, these intelligence efforts culminated in the Chain Murders (qatl-hayeh zanjire-i), a series of killings primarily targeting intellectuals and artists. Outside the country, from roughly 1987 to 1998, prominent dissident Iranians were assassinated by regime agents in high-profile incidents in Germany, Austria, and France. These assassinations still cast a long shadow in Iranian cultural memory, and such threats continue to affect Iranian diaspora communities to this day. So when our narrator Yadollah remarks that his fellow Iranians in exile "can't stand the sight of each other" and gossip about each other's possible connections to the Iranian regime, it is not a reflection of baseless paranoia, but rather a largely rational response to a terrifying and unsettling political context.

Woodwind Harmony rejects a number of trends in Iranian literature that were popular when Ghassemi was coming of age in the 1960s and 1970s, such as social realism, heavy-handed political symbolism, and commitment to dissenting against the Shah's authoritarianism. This so-called "committed" literature (adabiyat-e mote'ahhed) dominated the years leading up to the revolution, and is typified by writers such as Sadegh Chubak, Jalal Al-e Ahmad, Jamal Mirsadeghi, and Ahmad Mahmoud. Ghassemi, however, only engages with these political questions obliquely, and his work is more in line with early writers of the strange and uncanny, such as Sadegh Hedayat, Gholam-Hossein Sa'edi, Bahram Sadeghi, and Houshang Golshiri, who were pioneers of Iranian psychological fiction before the revolution. After the revolution, a certain niche developed for psychological fiction, including innovative and experimental narrative techniques, such as in the writings of Abbas Maroufi, Amir Hassan Cheheltan, and Bijan Najdi.

Woodwind Harmony's innovations in form and departure from traditional themes no doubt contributed to its broad appeal among Iranian readers. Ghassemi is best understood as a part of this new psychological movement, as well as having been deeply influenced by postmodern Western writers like Samuel Beckett and Italo Calvino. Reviewing the French translation, *Le Monde* critic Gérard Meudal called *Woodwind Harmony* "an unexpected union between *One Thousand and One Nights* and E.T.A. Hoffmann." Other readers have mentioned hearing echoes of Louis-Ferdinand Céline in its narrator's darkly humorous voice.

When I asked Ghassemi what background information he'd like to include here that Western readers might not know, he specifically referenced the vibrant international arts scene that was Iran in the 1970s. For example, from 1967 to 1977, the Shiraz Arts Festival was held annually in Shiraz and Persepolis, and lavishly funded by Queen Farah Pahlavi. This festival showcased Iranian theater, fiction, poetry, film, and music, but also attracted many artists from abroad. The result was a rich melting pot of Western and Iranian influences that propelled many artists' careers forward and helped them keep abreast of global trends. It is from this multicultural context that Ghassemi's novel emerged.

Another important element that makes Ghassemi's work stand out is his prose style, which, in Persian, grabs you straight away and draws you in. In his lectures on writing, Ghassemi speaks about his strategies for creating "magnetism" in prose, which he considers its most important quality. His sentences flow with a propulsive energy that drives the engine of the narrative forward. At the same time, his style marks itself as stylistically complex, and bristles with humorous undertones of irony and self-awareness.

Not to diminish my own efforts as a translator, but this is a style that tends to translate well into English. Due to a tendency in modern Persian fiction to favor plain, unstyled, and spare prose, literary translations from Persian into English can often come out flat. For instance, Persian does not require subjects at the beginning of the sentence to let us know who is doing what, or what is happening. The verb comes at the end of the sentence and tells us everything we need to know. As a result, a Persian text can give us fifty sentences in a row to the effect of "she said," "she walked," "she saw," "she sat down," and never once feel structurally repetitive. This is a recurring issue in Persian-to-English translation that I usually spend a lot of time and energy combatting—moving around clauses, adverbs of time, adverbs of motion, etc.—to artificially regenerate structural diversity in the English. In this regard, Ghassemi's complex prose is a dream to work with. It generally carries over into English in a stylized, almost flowery form that reads to us as immediately Literary with a capital "L."

That is not to say that this style presented no difficulties. I wouldn't say I was able to entirely throw off the yoke of that traditional adage espoused by translators everywhere—"English cannot handle long sentences." English can handle long sentences, but only in specific ways. It cannot, for example, easily accommodate four adverbs of time or place in a single clause, or five subordinate clauses in a single sentence (I may or may not be referring to a certain sentence on the first page of this novel, which I was forced to edit eighteen times and am still not particularly satisfied with). In some cases, I had to split Ghassemi's elaborate word-towers into two sentences, though I tried to avoid doing that wherever I could.

Another distinct element of Ghassemi's prose is the emphasis on sound. As a professional musician, he has a strong handle on rhythm and the qualities of sounds appearing in his text. Indeed, when reading his own work aloud, Ghassemi is extremely attuned to rhythm and meter. I noticed he reads in a particular style of declamation that is typically reserved for Persian poetry. This focus on sound is first hinted at in the novel's title, which the author told me alludes to the irony of a loud, blaring wind section attempting to play a soothing nocturne (a tranquil genre normally reserved for the strings, piano, or voice). This concept of a cacophonous harmonizing will become important later in the novel.

In general, Persian tends to be very nondescript in its sound verbs. The most common structures are to say a certain sound "came," "was heard," or "could be heard." Over the course of a novel, these descriptions begin to sound vague, imprecise, or just downright odd when translated literally into English. Ghassemi, however, fills his text with precise sound verbs. In *Woodwind Harmony*, sounds don't just "come," they clink, smash, shatter, grind, scrape, whirl, tap, squeak, knock, ring, pound, swell, creak, and rumble. Characters plod, scream, shuffle, chant, moan, stomp, howl, stumble, and groan. The discordant sounds of everyday life in cramped, thinly-walled rooms are reimagined as a grand symphony. I tried to reflect this element of Ghassemi's style by including musically-inflected verbs, such as a passage where I wrote "the grind of Bénédicte's saw crescendoed," rather than simply, "rose up" or "became loud" (boland shod).

The issue of characters' names in the text is another element which posed difficulties in translation. The novel features a large cast of secondary characters who make up the community of outcasts living in the ramshackle building owned by French communist and idealist Érik François Schmidt. Many of these characters go by several names or have nicknames, to the extent that even our narrator comments on his confusion. Some of these names seem to conform to the Iranian practice of having a more "Islamic" name for official documents and a more "Iranian" name or nickname for friends and family. For example, Fereydoon (an ancient Iranian name) is occasionally called Morteza, while Seyyed (an Islamic title reserved for descendants of Prophet Mohammad) has been known to go by Cyrus (the Iranian name of an Achaemenid king from pre-Islamic times). This confusion of naming is another way to add to the drama of the novel's core mystery, but also represents the theme of fragmented identity alluded to earlier.

All the Iranian characters have Islamic/Iranian names except for Yadollah's unhinged neighbor, Prophet. His name is written out phonetically in Persian script as "Pro-fet," as if borrowed directly from French prophète. It is unclear to me to what extent the meaning of this name would have been obvious to a Persian reader in the 1990s, when French and English literacy was not quite as common as it is now. Much Persian-language criticism on the novel glosses this point specifically, as if it could be missed by readers. That being said, Francophilia has a long history in Iran, as France was often viewed as the peak of literary, artistic, and intellectual culture from at least the 1920s onward. We can also imagine that an Iranian reader who picks up this work is already fairly literary-minded, and may well be aware of this important naming choice.

Returning to the theme of fragmentation, I faced many challenges in how to mark time jumps in the narrative, or whether to mark them at all. Since the original novel does not give the reader many extra clues on how to read it, I chose not to interfere too much in this regard either. However, a reader would do well to be on their guard. Paying close attention to shifts in tense can reveal a lot, as the narrator occasionally slips into present tense. These moments are critical to the development of the overall arc of the story. For the most part, non-linear junctures in the narrative are marked by numbered subchapter headings. However, the narrative occasionally indulges in flashback within flashback—such as when the narrator reads from his late father-in-law's diary—and these cases were primarily indicated by quotation marks, italics, or spacing in the text. I aimed to carefully preserve these distinctions through the spacing and punctuation. In other cases, the narrator launches into an extended backstory while being interrogated by the angels of death. The sudden reappearance of the angels, or a piece of dialogue, can occur with no warning. Ghassemi's background as a playwright may be illuminating here—he has a penchant for the theatrical and short scene-like vignettes.

Despite jumping around in time, space, life, and afterlife, the novel maintains a distinct focus on the word "now." A quick search of the translated manuscript reveals 172 instances of "now"—an average of more than one per page. This focus on the "now" is a reflection of the novel's interest in exploring the nature of memory. By featuring a narrator with the time gap disease and a main character, Mathilde, who no longer has access to short term memories for more than a minute or so, Ghassemi zeroes in on the unreliable nature of human perception. All of this serves to underline his primary theme of the trauma of displacement and the story of a life shattered by exile.

In addition to the narrator's interrogators—the Islamic angels of death—the reader will encounter a few other references to Islamic cosmology, which may benefit from some background explanation. In particular, Yadollah relies on several stock images to allude to the worst punishments of the afterlife. First is the threat that he will be thrown to the Ghashiye serpent, a giant snake of the underworld referenced in the Quran, who viciously attacks sinners.

Second, he references the brains of the sinner, which are said to be boiled in a cauldron, and then consumed by the Ghashiye serpent. Finally, he mentions the evil-doers and recalls visions of their bodies being gruesomely sawn in half.

The narrator himself suggests that these images have been put in his head by the naqqāl, or the traditional storyteller, who travelled around reciting important Iranian and Islamic legends. The naqqāl was particularly associated with the coffeehouse in the seventeenth through early twentieth centuries. He would typically be accompanied by a portable mural containing images of important characters, action sequences, and sometimes grisly death scenes. For example, it might include characters from Ferdowsi's eleventh-century Book of Kings (referenced in the novel's epigraph), such as Jamshid. A virtuous and mythical king who reigns justly for seven hundred years, Jamshid is eventually tempted into hubris and brutally sawn in half by Zahhak, a tyrannical king controlled by the devil Iblis. Additionally, within Islamic tradition, the fourth Islamic caliph, Imam Ali, is often represented as slicing his enemies in half with his notoriously sharp sword. It is these scenes that are conjured for Iranian readers when they read about Prophet's apocalyptic paintings on the walls of his room, and what our narrator has in mind when he imagines the punishments of hell.

There are many people to thank for helping to bring about this translation, not least of which is Reza Ghassemi, who graciously entrusted me with his novel and answered all of my questions in detail over the course of several meetings. This translation would not have been possible without the invaluable support of the Mo Habib Translation Prize, the judges' trust in my work, the University of Washington, Seattle, and Aria Fani's tireless efforts to establish and manage the prize. Most of all, I am greatly indebted to the editors at Deep Vellum and their dedication to bringing world literature to English readers. On a personal level, I have many people to thank, including my first and most important readers, Betty Long, Anna Learn, Victoria Plutshack, and Laura Quay. My colleagues Parisa Saranj and Mehrdad Babadi patiently explained numerous intricacies of the novel's prose. I am also grateful to Nazee Nowroozi, my friend and Persian teacher, for the countless hours she spent with me, refining my understanding of the subtleties of this Persian text. Finally, I dedicate this translation to my mentors Michael Henry Heim and Franklin Lewis, who first inspired me to embark on the path of literary translation.

Michelle Quay
April 2025

Cast of Characters

Residents of the Sixth Floor

Yadollah	An Iranian immigrant in 1990s Paris. Narrator of the story
Seyyed Alexander	Narrator's close friend and rival (in chess, life, and love)
Ra'na	An Iranian girl who has recently immigrated. Temporarily staying in the narrator's kitchen
Prophet	A disturbed Iranian neighbor who pulls a knife on Seyyed
Fereydoon	An Iranian carpenter
Bénédicte	A Frenchwoman and unofficial "captain" of the floor
Kalantar	Iranian tough guy and archnemesis of Seyyed. Ally of Prophet
Jean	A young, shy French intellectual type. Dating Emmanuelle who lives on the fourth floor
Milosh	A Czech immigrant who plays the cello
Bernard	Narrator's friend who tries to get him a singing job
Ali	A new convert to Islamic mysticism. Ally of Prophet

Supernatural Beings

Nakeer & Monkar	The angels of death according to Islam. They appear in the form of "Murnau's Faust" and "The Native American from *One Flew Over the Cuckoo's Nest*"
The Ghashiye Serpent	A giant snake of the Underworld
The Shadow	A mysterious shadow that "usurped the narrator's place" after he lost his beloved at fourteen

The Landlord and his family

Érik François Schmidt	Elderly and idealistic French landlord of the building. Holocaust survivor
Mathilde	Érik François Schmidt's wife, who has dementia
Érik François Schmidt Jr.	The landlord's son, a skinny and frail "poet" who lives on the fourth floor
Gabik	Érik and Mathilde's big black dog

Narrator's family and friends

Narrator's wife	Killed in a train crash prior to the events of the narrative
Khatoun	Narrator's mother-in-law
The ex-officer	Narrator's father-in-law, who left the narrator his memoirs
Narrator's daughter	Taken in by a cult leader, never to be seen again
M.A.R.	Narrator's ex, who apparently had his child without him knowing
Narrator's son	Shows up to confront the narrator

Other minor figures

Mehdi	Former sixth floor resident
Taqi	Former sixth floor resident, who used to live in the narrator's rooms
Agnès	Seyyed's wife, a Frenchwoman
Ingrid	Fellow musician who has a crush on the narrator

Woodwind Harmony in the Nighttime

When a man's fortune grows dim,
All his efforts bring naught to him.
—*Ferdowsi*

CHAPTER ONE

No Gabik, not here!

-1-

I was like a horse that had sensed impending disaster. You've seen how their eyes bug out, right? How they snort the fear swirling around in their skulls out their trembling nostrils? How they whinny and stomp their hooves?

No, I haven't seen it either. But if I were a horse, that's how I'd express my terror. (Who knows? Anything is possible. Maybe one day, in the damp corner of an empty mud brick stable, in the half-light suffused with the smell of hay and dung, one of my ancestors placed a stool under the belly of a four-legged beast so she could conceive my embryo, infusing it permanently with a sense of desperation and longing.)

But I neither whinnied nor stomped my hooves. I ran down the stairs in a flash, taking them a few at a time, and rang the bell for the fourth floor.

I knew that Mathilde, the landlord's elderly wife, would come to the door and examine me carefully through the peephole. Then when she opened the door, her startled eyes would lock onto mine, bulging out of their sockets like she'd just witnessed something terrifying. With a kind smile, she would wait for me to tell her why I was there. When I told her, for the twelfth time in the past year of my residence here, I'd come to pay my rent (though this time I was lying), for the twelfth time she would ask where I lived. For the twelfth time, I'd have to tell her on the top floor. After a short stroll down the empty, deserted corridors of her memory, Mathilde would slowly do a little half-turn and make way for me, either because she didn't trust her mind or because she trusted her big black dog Gabik so much.

I'd walk into the hallway of the dimly-lit apartment and once again it would hurt my pride a little that she didn't remember me. Then I'd console myself by thinking that when time stops for a person, there is no space left in their mind, however small; not for me or anybody else. All that remains are some fibers—assembled from the ashes of anxious confusion—that form tangled neural networks and bury time in their own circuitry. You've seen Hiroshima after the bomb, right? Those clocks with the melted coils? No, it really shouldn't have gotten to me. This melted second hand eternally fixed on a single moment, Mathilde, was no longer a living creature but the faded image of a woman who, in a manner of speaking, had whinnied and stomped her hooves out of fright on that foggy, rainy morning of April 1943, when the camera's shutter opened to record her image.

I pressed the buzzer with my thumb and waited. From the sixth floor, the sound of Milosh's cello, sonorous and impassioned, reverberated in the stairwell and made the smoke wafting out of Fereydoon's room swirl like a trembling cloud.

"Don't tell me they're not home."

Just as I pressed down hard on the buzzer, I sensed something beginning to grow inside me. Something like a hideous and terrifying monster. I felt disgusted with myself.

Damn my luck! Couldn't Érik François Schmidt have refused to take pity on Prophet? Couldn't Prophet have been that same timid young man he was at first?

I'd spent my entire life in the Eastern Hemisphere aligning my schedule with the Western Hemisphere, so when it got dark, the sixth floor of this building became like a small planet for me, of which I was the sole captain. No one had any complaints about this. Mind you, in this city, where everything is condemned to obey the all-powerful silence of the walls and no one is even allowed to flush their toilet from ten o'clock onwards, there were so many noise complaints wherever I had lived before, I was obliged to pack up everything and move somewhere else.

Here, I had been at such peace over the past year, I told myself even if this small attic room had its drawbacks, it was the best place in the world for someone like me whose life was twelve hours off from everyone else's.

Shame that peace couldn't last. Suddenly, a stranger's face appeared on my little planet and changed everyone's destiny.

The first time I saw him was on an August afternoon. Usually, I go to bed at seven in the morning and get up around two in the afternoon. On that day, even though the strange sounds emanating from the room next door had woken me up hours ago, I still couldn't get up before my usual time, though I was very curious. When I opened my door, I was shocked. It looked like there'd been a coup. In a total departure from normal events, the door to the room next to mine was open and an odd sound was coming from the stairwell. I was staring in confusion at the junk strewn everywhere, the dirt covering the hallway floor and the hardwood stairs when he appeared. He was relatively tall, with an athletic build. He said hello very quickly, traversed the length of the hallway in a rush, and went into the room next door to mine.

As I headed toward the kitchen, a note on the wall caught my eye: "My cat will have to be loose in the hall today, I apologize in advance."

Without thinking, I turned my head to look down the hallway. The stranger emerged from the room next door, carrying a large wooden table with a broken leg, and quickly descended the stairs.

I took the note off the wall and went into my kitchen, which was to the right of the staircase.

The bell of the Saint-Paul Saint-Louis Church rang out fourteen times, and I sensed that my small planet had left its orbit.

-2-

I wasn't asleep—that much I'm sure of—since I could feel the knife sticking out my back. I also sensed the rank smell of dried blood covering my entire body. So where was this slanted light coming from?

He had an eerie resemblance to Gary Cooper. The only difference was his hair, which—unlike Gary Cooper's—was long and a little messy. The slanted light illuminated only the right half of his face, lending him a ghostly quality that immediately reminded me of German expressionist cinema, particularly Murnau's *Faust*.

What had completely thrown me for a loop was this slanted light. If he was standing outside the cramped, dark space I was in, why was the light completely localized to his face? And if he was inside the space with me, then . . .

It didn't make sense. Surely it wasn't possible for a single room to have two different spatial fields inside of it? And then, one light and one dark?

Murnau's Faust had been calmly and quietly reviewing a ledger he had with him, and now paused on a single point for some time.

I held my breath and waited for him to start interrogating me. But, it seemed that's not what he had in mind this early on. Or maybe this was just a little gamesmanship to try to break down my resistance. Now, why he thought I was planning to resist, I can't say.

Truth be told, I'd already decided to tell him everything. It wasn't my fault that I went pale at the sound of a shout, or wet myself if someone got slapped. I was raised to be afraid. Of everything. Of elders, that they'd be offended; of children, that their hearts would break; of friends, that they'd get upset and desert me; of enemies, that they'd be provoked and attack me.

One of the poets said, "Don't reveal your secrets to anyone. I have oft seen companions that were spies."

Another said, "Don't gossip near the wall. There might be ears on the other side."

"Don't put rocks on top of a wall, or they may fall on you."

"Don't build your house in the path of the flood, slave."

"Don't look at something wonderful and assume there's disaster up ahead."

"Don't make hard work your master."

You get the idea. All of it was advice, all in the negative, and no one ever said what you *should* do. Another one said, "You who are capable, do something, before you are incapable of doing anything," and in the end, didn't say what that 'something' was. This is how I ended up learning nothing, including how to resist.

Murnau's Faust still had his nose in his ledger. The silence and waiting were suffocating. Without warning, something that had been locked away behind my gritted teeth sprung out of my mouth: "I was always told there were two angels of death!"

An even more distressing silence was laid atop the first. Suddenly, I sensed a gaping abyss was opening up between us. I searched for an appropriate sentence to save myself from falling into this terrifying chasm, which grew deeper and deeper with dizzying speed. But only bits of advice paraded themselves before my eyes. I saw my father's mouth moving in anger, my mother's mouth, my aunts' mouths, my teacher's mouth, my boss's mouth. I was falling headfirst when a gentle sound reverberated in the space and snapped the abyss back from its depth.

"Poor thing!"

Murnau's Faust, who so far had been preoccupied with his own work, glanced at his partner (there was no one beside him, but he looked over the way a person can only when they're looking at someone). Pressing the ledger against his chest, he said, "It seems you had a particular issue in life."

Though I had never been a person without issues, no matter how I tried to recall what problem I'd had in life, nothing came to mind in that moment. Suddenly, for no particular reason, a whimsical feeling came over me, "An issue, you say?"

"Yes, an issue."

A familiar voice from beside Faust added in a mild tone, "A particular issue!"

Fear gripped me. I realized a few things at once. First, that Faust wasn't alone; he had a partner. Second, that this partner was invisible to the eye. And third, what he meant by "a particular issue."

"I'm sorry," I said, "Which one are you?"

"What do you mean 'which one?'" said Faust. "Just answer the questions!"

"Look Mr . . ." I said.

"Say whichever one you like, it makes no difference," said the partner.

"I can't see you," I replied. "I have to address him. If he would be so kind as to . . ."

"It doesn't matter. We work together," said the partner.

"Look Mr . . ." I said.

"Why are you smiling?"

This was Murnau's Faust who had snapped at me. I cleared my throat and said incoherently, "Well you see, you know, it's just that . . ."

"It's just that what?"

"It's just that . . . your name . . ."

"What's wrong with my name?"

I was used to addressing my listeners by name. The name was

like a needle which drew the thread of my thoughts behind it and gave them order. The question that had been posed, however, made me completely lose my train of thought. So, instead of finishing what I was going to say, I blurted out: "You speak our language!"

"A distracted mind! It's been noted here."

"It's so surprising. You have every power in the universe at your disposal, so why do you need two for this job?"

I didn't mean for things to go this far, but I couldn't help it. I'd stumbled onto a slippery slope and there was no way to save myself from plummeting down it.

Faust looked me straight in the eye and said, "Five and a half billion people on Earth—how many do you think speak your shit language? Thirty million? Fifty million? Sixty?"

First, I wanted to say that our language wasn't shit; Mr. Jamalzadeh said it was sweet as sugar. Second, some people may have disagreed, but they didn't say it was shit; they said it was like a sugar cube. Plus, it's a language that's been all over. They say it even made it to Bengal. But I realized I'd hurt Faust pretty badly. I had to skirt around the issue so things wouldn't get any worse than they already were. An appropriate sentence came to mind that I could use to help smooth things over a bit. I cleared my throat: "Look Mr . . ." But I couldn't go on. The hint of a smile was spreading quickly over my face. What madness was this—to start my sentence with this dangerous opening gesture?

Even if my silence was broken in a way that wasn't terribly awkward, it was still humiliating in and of itself. My very awareness of this fact left me defenseless against the bomb that was about to go off. Suddenly, the dam inside me burst and the reverberations of my obnoxious laughter made the steady pillars of light begin to quake.

-3-

Why now? Exactly a month and a half after the night of the incident? Why didn't I come that very night? At least the police could have been informed. What a disaster! I'd let the poison of that event slowly build and now, brimming over with panic, I stood on the brink of madness, taking the stairs several at a time to tell my landlord something I should have told him that night. I shouldn't have let things get so out of hand.

As I pressed the buzzer, I steeled myself so when I came face to face with old Érik François Schmidt on his doorstep (after making repetitive, mind-numbing small talk with Mathilde), this time, just this once, I wouldn't let my gaze fall on his strange nose like it always did. I had paid my rent a few days before and had to stock up every ounce of willpower to do something that seemed to grow more and more impossible as time went on. I had to shout something into the ears of this nearly-deaf old man, when even whispering it could cost me my life.

"Don't tell me he's out of town."

If only I'd come that day. The day I saw Prophet for the first time in the stairwell, with his round, bulging eyes, like an ominous raven. He exuded such raw power, like a dagger that could slice the air. He took the six flights of stairs up and down with no breaks, and each time he brought down with him a table, bed, or other piece of dusty, used furniture.

This move-in, which was unfolding in a rather unusual way, was a clear sign of the catastrophe that awaited. But I was stunned by something else: a hundred times . . . a hundred and one . . . a hundred and two . . .

I'd left the kitchen and headed back to my room, and still, I was counting without realizing it: a hundred and twenty one times . . . a hundred and twenty two . . .

Where did all this energy come from? When I came up the stairs carrying nothing, I'd start coughing from the third floor on. My knees began to tremble and I couldn't see straight. And now: a hundred and twenty three . . . a hundred and twenty four . . . and he wasn't even breathing hard!

It was eight o'clock when he finished emptying the room that shared a wall with mine. I realized this when the noise of his rustling around settled down, and when the smell of sautéed onions came wafting in through the door.

How could he possibly have convinced the poor old landlord? How did he manage to pry this room—the building's storage room, which many residents were gunning for—out of the landlord's clutches?

That means . . .

The day Prophet came to our floor, Seyyed and I mourned. My room shared a wall with Prophet's, and Seyyed was right across from him. It didn't seem like he was a night owl like us. The way he looked and moved was different, not like us exiles and immigrants. He could have been an army sergeant, a construction worker, or a mechanic, something along those lines. If he was one of those early-to-bed, early-to-rise folks, we were going to be in trouble. Plus, if, like the French, he didn't so much as make a peep in his room, he'd get fed up and complain after a couple of days of putting up with our noise.

But our worries turned out to be unfounded; it quickly became clear he was a night owl too. I figured that out from the light that shone through the crack under his door and the sound of his occasional cough. Now, what a person like him did all night cooped up inside his room was another question entirely. In any case, he was a secretive kind of guy. He rarely came out of his room, and when he did, it was only to use the restroom or get some water out of the bathroom sink, the sole point of confluence between the residents of this remote planet. By which I mean the sixth floor of the building that belonged to Érik François Schmidt, an eighty-nine-year-old doctor living on the fourth floor who had spent his entire life fighting for a just world, and finally, now that that had failed, consoled himself with realizing that dream world in the only domain over which he retained authority: the six-story building which at this very moment, enveloped in the strong odor of sautéed onions, was slowly but surely headed for disaster.

-4-

Murnau's Faust was flipping through his notebook in absolute silence. A silence more terrifying than an out-and-out attack. I knew my pointless drivel and idiotic laughter would be my undoing in the end. That night in the village of Doost-Mohammad, we were sitting on the mud brick terrace, hemmed in on all sides by night and desert, and Bahram Nawruy, taking his lute in hand, struck up a tune in a language I didn't understand a word of. I was bewitched, speechless, drowning in the torpor of the evening stars that made me feel I was dead. The enchanting voice was not the Balochi singer's; it was the voice of Nakeer and Monkar, the angels of death, who read out the register of my deeds. One with music and the other with words. I saw that there was no reproach here, not even blame. I watched as they counted my sins, but not with contempt. It was all done with pity, as if to say, if he slipped, he slipped, but not from weakness; if he erred, he erred, but not by choice.

How weightless I felt that evening. I said to myself, "So this is death? This sweetness lying in wait?"

What a vision I had of this night compared to how it turned out in the end! Bernard was right when he wrote me that bitter, reproachful letter accusing me of self-destructive behavior. Poor thing, what trouble he'd gone to in order to give me the chance to find some kind of freedom from this mongrel existence. How could he know that at precisely the wrong moment, I'd purposefully shoot myself in the foot? I wished he'd forgive me. How could I tell him that it wasn't within my control? That in actuality it's somebody else doing the shooting? More than that even—that it's me, but I'm shooting at someone else? How can I tell Bernard that a man in the desert always lives with his shadow? Everywhere he goes, his shadow is there with him, right or left. Everywhere he goes, he follows his shadow or drags it along behind him. He is only free from his shadow for one moment, just for a single moment: high noon. When the lances of the sun's rays strike the crown of the head.

And yet, he is still not alone in this moment. For a desert man, the only possession of value is his shadow. When he sits, it sits with him. When he stands, it stands too. In the morning, it stretches its height to the western horizon. In the evening, it stretches to the east. What human is that loyal? Would you let a friend like that get burned when the sunlight daggers shone down? You see how the shadow collapses in on itself. How it tags along at your feet. You let it slip under your toenails into yourself. It's become second nature, since this is the least you can do for it. When it's well-ensconced inside your body, the sun's daggers retreat. Then, little by little, it drags itself out from under your toenails. But what if it doesn't?

That was exactly the misfortune that befell me on a summer's day in 1968. I was standing there, as usual, waiting for Somaylu to show up carrying my beloved's letter. It just took a few moments, a few seconds of the sun's rays shining directly on my head. I was fourteen years old. So young.

When Somaylu arrived empty-handed, his teeth clenched and a glistening wetness swirling in the whirlpool of his dark eyes, my entire being was rattled by a tremendous earthquake. Somaylu ran, his grief erupting like a volcano. He fled and sobbed, and I, thunderstruck, unable to react, saw with my own eyes that my shadow had retreated within me. This time, it pulled me out from under my toenails instead.

You see, Bernard, you're allowed to call me "self-destructive," but I'm not allowed to tell anyone that the reason I'm always fighting with myself, the reason I'm always acting against my own best interest, is that I'm not really myself. That these shots I fire into my own foot are really shots aimed at my shadow. A shadow that usurped me and has sat angrily in my place for years.

-5-

O dear naïve Érik François! If only you'd been a tyrant, or had a heart made of stone like so many other people. Then the sixth floor of your building wouldn't have become our refuge. Then you wouldn't have given the room next door—which for years had been used as a storage room—to Prophet free of charge. Then we wouldn't have clung so tightly to those attic rooms despite our poverty and misery, or at least, after that awful night of September 17th, we would have packed up our things and decamped to another ramshackle place somewhere else. Or, if you were a tyrant, what would we be doing there at all? We considered those rooms manna from heaven. Where could we have gone that people wouldn't give us trouble for the color of our skin or our nationality? Where could we go that they wouldn't ask us for residency permits? Where they didn't charge more for rent than we could afford? You didn't ask anyone for a security deposit. You didn't ask anyone for proof of income.

That's how we ended up here long-term. That's why, on that horrible night of September 17th, when Prophet kicked down Seyyed's door and held a knife to his throat, the only thing we didn't think of was simply to give up the rooms.

Seyyed and I were coming back from a night out. We had dinner at a Mexican restaurant that served good, fairly cheap food. Cheerful and tipsy on tequila, we came home so each could go about his nightly business. Seyyed would work on a story, the principal hero of which was yours truly; and I would work on a portrait, which I painted of Érik François Schmidt *in absentia*. Of course, painting wasn't my actual job. I couldn't sleep at night, and if I didn't keep myself busy with something, I'd go crazy. Nothing worked better than painting. Plus, anything I didn't understand, I had to paint to comprehend. That's why I started my portrait of Érik François Schmidt. I wanted to understand the secret of his bizarre nose, which was huge and had fleshy protrusions jutting out from each nostril, one the size of a walnut and the other a hazelnut, day by day continuing to grow.

We'd arrived just a few minutes ago. Silence hovered over the building. There was no sign of Milosh's cello, Ali's mystical chanting, or the moans of Kalantar's wife.

Seyyed had returned to his room, and I was making small talk with Ra'na as I changed.

Ra'na was obviously unhappy, but she tried to hide her wounded pride behind a plastered-on smile. It had been about a month since she'd come to stay with me. She called first. I picked up the phone and heard her trembling voice.

"Can I come stay with you for a few days?"

It didn't occur to me that she'd gotten herself in trouble again. (She was young and pretty. Of course whoever she went to stay with would be drawn to her. So eventually, she got into some sticky situations. After a few days of putting up with her host's idiotic advances, she was forced to pack her pure and wholesome essence in her suitcase and go somewhere else.) Of course, I also didn't reflect on why she always went somewhere where her host just happened to be single. Instead I said to myself, "Witness the hands of Fate at work!"

This wasn't the first time I'd privileged a belief in fate over logic. Last year she came and stayed with me for a while. When I heard her voice on the other end of the line saying, "I'm sorry, I took down this number, but I forgot to write down whose it was . . .", I said to myself, "Witness the hands of Fate at work!"

I moved my easel and canvas to the center of the room. I wanted to get to work, but Ra'na wasn't planning on going anywhere. She just sat on the edge of the bed, bitter and with furrowed brows. The tipsiness from the tequila was turning sour. As I mindlessly dabbled with the paints, searching for a way out of this situation, suddenly there came the loud crack of something getting broken in the hallway. At first, I paid it no mind. When the noise grew louder, Ra'na and I looked at each other.

"That damned woman again?" she sneered.

Who else could it be? From morning to midnight, Bénédicte was the captain of this ship, and from midnight onward, I was.

Unconsciously my hand drifted toward the lock on the door, but I very quickly pulled away. I had known Bénédicte a long time, ever since those days I was living with my wife (may she rest in peace). Most nights, I went over to Seyyed's to try to numb the pain of the defeats I'd sustained in life with the taste of victory on the chessboard, a place where battles had meaning and seemed more real.

Bénédicte lived in Room 6, right across from the stairwell. The fact that her room didn't face anyone's was considered a real drawback, and in order to make up for it, she was forced to drag her business out into the hallway from time to time. I was the only person who could potentially be considered her neighbor across the hall, since Rooms 1 and 12 were mine. But, unfortunately for her, a wide stairwell wedged a large gap between them. One of my rooms was on the right side of the stairwell, the other on the left. Even though it was physically impossible, I wouldn't have minded if one day her wish came true and these separated rooms were joined. That way, even if one of my rooms was directly across from hers, I would at least be able to open the doors between my rooms, like Seyyed did, and wouldn't have to lock and unlock doors a hundred times a day, which would be a godsend. And maybe in that case, many of the little shows Bénédicte put on in the hallway would be called off. Wasn't the whole point of all this racket for one of the neighbors across the hall to stick his head out?

As for me, my situation was clear. Room 2 had been the building storage room for years, and now that it had become residential, they gave it to a person like Prophet, who always kept his door closed and never came out except to carry out his bodily functions. Room 11, which was next to my kitchen, belonged to one of those new-age types, a fellow Iranian called Ali. He lived on the same side of the hall as Bénédicte and used Room 11 as a kitchen. Then there was the bathroom, and finally, at the end of the hall was Room 10, which belonged to a young musician from Czechoslovakia named Milosh. His room was far enough away that it didn't matter if it was across the hall or on the same side as Bénédicte's.

"She gone off the rails again?" When Ra'na got upset, her hands trembled.

"Don't pay her any attention," I said.

The noise intensified more than ever before. It sounded like someone was taking an axe to wooden tables and chairs. Ra'na got up. She stood listening for a moment, and then, with the dread of a mother who suddenly realizes her child teeters on the edge of the pool (or, since Seyyed and Ra'na were too close in age for this expression to really work, let me try it again with a little adjustment: 'with the dread of a woman who suddenly realizes her husband teeters on the edge of the pool') she lunged for the door. I grabbed her arm: "What are you doing?"

"It sounded like Seyyed's voice!"

Standing there with her arm firmly in my grip, I listened for a moment, and then carefully unlatched the door.

Ra'na turned back toward me in terror.

"He's calling for you!" she said, pushing past me. I was frozen, but she dashed outside.

A voice was calling me, as though from the bottom of a well.

-6-

Milosh played with such intensity, it seemed like the smoke coiling up the stairwell emanated from his bow. Losing hope, I decided to press the buzzer for the last time. Suddenly the door made a sound and Gabik appeared before me in the blink of an eye, as usual. He reared up on his hind legs and laid his front paws on my shoulders, while his huge, bulging eyes stared directly into mine.

Panicked, I was damp with sweat. Gabik, who seemed particularly peeved by what was happening on the sixth floor, was rubbing his nose wildly against my face. I held myself perfectly still, lest he rip off my nose with a single jump.

I wasn't afraid of the dog. Or at least, for a while now I hadn't been scared out of my mind when I saw him, or disgusted when I touched him. Of course, getting to this point wasn't easy. In the culture I grew up with, dogs were unclean creatures, and the slightest brush against one meant you were contaminated. You couldn't stand it until you had a chance to perform ablutions. Worse still, if people wanted to curse you, they'd turn you into a dog. There were people who had committed so many sins that they'd been reincarnated as a dog after their death.

With this sort of upbringing, getting along with dogs was no mean feat, even if you hadn't really believed in any of it for a long time. But things were resolved quite simply. One night, sometime after I had grown accustomed to the constant presence of dogs (or, perhaps more accurately, the dogs had grown accustomed to the constant presence of me), I came across a small dog with curly hair that bore a strange resemblance to a lamb. With no hesitation, I ran forward and gathered it into my arms. At that moment, I realized that even if I no longer held onto those old beliefs, the form of them stuck with me. In other words, I hated dogs so long as they looked like dogs. Similarly, I had previously harbored a similar hatred for goats, since they were really just sheep that looked like dogs. Since I could now see dogs with curly hair as lambs, why couldn't I see dogs with straight hair as goats?

With this stratagem in mind, I was eventually able to cultivate a sort of friendly feeling toward my friends and acquaintances' dogs, to the extent that we were on kissing terms. But I was still afraid of Gabik, for a few reasons. First, he was enormous, and if I weren't afraid, you'd wonder. Second, he'd been a stray and could be aggressive. Third, he was entirely black, and for that reason he was more likely than any other canine to be a cursed human in the form of a dog. Especially since I'd seen something about his eyes that led me to believe he wasn't really a dog. Fourth—and this was strangest of all—Gabik was both himself and not. How can I explain? Over the course of my one-year stay, he'd died and come back to life many times. It's a little difficult to explain, but I will. Practically every time I went to my landlord to pay rent—after recovering a bit from that first little ritual by the door—I would decide to pet Gabik, who kept running circles around me, trying to establish neighborly ties of affection. Yet, every time, as soon as I said, "Gabik," the landlord's wife responded with her perennially compassionate smile, "This isn't Gabik."

"But you were calling him Gabik."

"Gabik's dead. This one is called Mouro."

Another time she said, "Gabik's dead. This is Wolf."

And another, "Gabik's dead, this is Bobby."

And another, "Gabik's dead, this is Rocky."

One day I lost my patience for this whole situation and said, "But this is the same dog I always see!"

"Since we loved Gabik so much, we tried to find a dog that looked like him."

Then, she rose slowly from her seat, picked up a picture off the shelf, and showed it to me. "This is Gabik. See?" I supposed she meant to say, "Don't you see how similar they look?" But just as she held the picture up for me, she froze, and stared into space. Then she resumed her sentence, "Isn't he so adorable?"

"But every morning when Mr. Schmidt drags him outside, I hear him from inside my room as he yells, 'No Gabik! Not here!'"

I think the last sentence, which I'd delivered in a loud impression of Schmidt, made him look up from his desk where he was busily writing out notices that rent payment was due. With a sheepish smile, as if he'd done something wrong, he said, "You know, he's a stray. He's not used to an apartment."

His wife had added apologetically, "No matter how much Érik yells at him, it makes no difference. He still pees in the stairwell."

My whole body began to tremble. Standing in front of the door and blocking Gabik's way out, Mathilde turned her startled eyes on me.

-7-

The door to Seyyed's room was wide open. My stomach dropped. Nobody on this floor ever left their doors open; not him, not anybody. Except for Kalantar, and everyone got mad at him for doing it.

The second I got to Seyyed's room, I was faced with a scene the likes of which I never could have imagined. Seyyed was on the ground and Prophet, shirtless, held a knife to his throat.

Seyyed Alexander was a good-looking young man who lived in Rooms 3 and 4, right across from Prophet. Anyone who saw him was immediately drawn to him. One of his friends swore he had some kind of magic charm. Of course, I'm not prepared to make such a claim, but I won't deny there was a certain magnetism about him. He was handsome and his pleasant smile, always on his face, was like a door open to heaven in those dark days when most people were bitter and depressed.

All he had to do was enter a room full of people. From the first minute he was chatting with you, and after half an hour it was like you'd been friends for a thousand years. Naturally, in my case, it was a little bit different. It took two years. I'm really not one for making friends, anyway. All it took was a single episode of my time gap disease for an instant animosity to take root between me and whoever I was talking to. Even worse, nothing interested me. I'd grown so detached that if someone at a party said excitedly, "Alexandre Dumas Sr. is the elder brother of Alexandre Dumas Jr. and the nephew of Roland Dumas, the Foreign Minister," or if they said, "A woman's genitalia are square," I wouldn't have batted an eye. What did it matter? Were they wrong? So? Let them be wrong. Why should I have to point out their error anyway? To show them and everybody else

I know better? Well, what would that change? Make me the center of attention? Of what use to me was other people's attention when, even over the course of a short conversation, the time gaps came for me dozens of times? Then I had to nod my head idiotically like a goat so the other person would think I was listening. Now, if they asked me something that required a negative answer, and I, suffering from one of my time gaps, nodded my head yes, how was I supposed to deal with their shock? Really, did I have to be insane to expose myself to this ordeal of listening to stories when, most of the time, I grasped neither the subject, the time, or the place of its occurrence? How was my company any different than that of an elevator operator, who was constantly in danger of hearing stories and missing out on the beginning or the end? At least no one expects a response from the elevator operator. In fact, people would be happy if his attention were engaged elsewhere.

Seyyed was the polar opposite of me. He would listen with total interest. Very often, he made subtle points in response to what other people were saying, showing the depth of his attention. That's how he always discovered possibilities in people that were essential to their development, even if they themselves were of little interest. But still, Seyyed hadn't made anything of himself in life, and neither had I. In this way, we were eerily similar. We were so different from each other, we'd actually grown alike. The way that night—in the depths of its being night—turns to day. We both squandered our own opportunities. The difference being that I did it by the untimely self-sabotage I mounted against my own good fortune, while he did it by creating too many opportunities and abandoning them in favor of new ones. Not a day went by when he didn't meet dozens of new people, and there was no one he couldn't derive some kind of mutual benefit from. This is how he ended up hopping from branch to branch. I too was constantly moving from branch to branch, but it was because none of the prospects held any appeal for me. If he moved on, it was because he spotted some more appealing prospect. He wrote poetry for a bit. He took lessons to learn to play the kamancheh. For a little while he bought and sold paintings and antiques. At one point he ran a restaurant. Sometimes he would sell carpets. Another time he was studying sociology. He studied some psychology too. He left all these things behind and took up writing. Then, not having made any real progress with that, he went back to selling carpets. This time, though, it was with a grand, ambitious plan to start a chain of carpet showrooms in different cities.

"Kilims and carpets are works of art. They belong on the wall, not on the floor!"

After all this hopping back and forth between branches, however, there was one constant that never changed: his never-ending pursuit of greatness. Insignificance had no place in Seyyed's spirit. He hated every mean thing, every mean bit of work, every mean little income or mean pedigree; in a word, he loathed anything that didn't have an air of greatness. Anyone who saw his pride in his country would say, "If our nation had a leader like that, what would it lack?"

He saw greatness not just in himself but in everyone. He didn't just want it for himself; he wanted it for everyone. With this outlook, it was no wonder he introduced me, a simple house painter, as the greatest painter in the country, and himself as one of the residents of Qom, the name of an Iranian city which suddenly became "Rome" when pronounced with a French accent.

That's why, the day he changed his nationality, he gave himself the name "Alexander." Eventually, he even produced a family tree from his father's heirlooms that showed he was descended from Italian nobility.

-8-

Murnau's Faust, disregarding my idiotic laughter, was looking at his notebook as though he'd just spotted something new in it. Under the slanted light, which was shining from the left, his well-shaven face took on a silvery sheen; his fair hair and white scarf were tossed softly in a breeze that wafted by. He snapped his notebook shut and turned to say something to his companion in a language I didn't understand. It sounded more like Balouchi than Arabic. Instantly, a piece of paper appeared in the air. Faust reached his hand out toward his friend—whose presence had now acquired its *raison d'être* like an "unseen" character in Kabuki theater—took the paper from him and turned to me.

"Is this your handwriting?"

"You know I can't read without my glasses."

Faust drew back his hand: "I'll read it for you."

A tiny ray of hope opened in my heart—so they didn't know everything after all! I could hide some things if I had to. In reality, my eyes were poor, but not so poor that I couldn't read anything without glasses.

Faust cleared his throat. "At the top of the page you wrote: 'Notes.' Then, you continued: 'Who is the murderer? Seyyed Alexander? A son I have with M.A.R.? The maniac next door? Or Khatoun, a woman who is the harbinger of death wherever she goes?' Then there are a few sentences that you've crossed out, but I'll read them anyway. You wrote, 'I have three serious diseases: time gaps, self-destructive tendencies, and the mirror illness. I will die twice, once by the hand of my son, who will kill my shadow, and another time by the hand of . . . (illegible). The first part is addressed to my son, the second part to the angels of death, Nakeer and Monkar, and the third part . . .' Aren't these your notes?"

I felt a knot in the pit of my stomach. These notes had to do with a book I'd written ages ago but had never published. Every publisher I sent it to said bluntly, "These ramblings are not literature and I've wasted my time." Since I'm the kind of person who always thinks other people are right, I decided not to waste my time either and turned to painting. That is, at first I painted buildings to make ends meet, then later, since I always had a bit of extra paint lying around anyway, I started painting portraits of people who puzzled me, just as a hobby. I began, first and foremost, with the portraits of a few publishers.

And now . . . they brushed aside an entire lifetime and instead got hung up on this book?

"As you know," I said, "I once took up the pen, for a time. Then, after I'd failed at that like I failed at so many other things . . ."

"Don't get off topic! Did you write this?"

"Yes, I did."

"You confirm that these notes belong to a book by the name of *Woodwind Harmony in the Nighttime,* which you published under a pseudonym?"

"No, that's not true. The book was never published."

"That's the same answer you gave in the book!" said Faust's partner.

"You asked the same question!" I replied.

"Do you confirm your previous answer?" asked Faust.

I told myself I had to set the precedent right from the beginning. What more could they do to me? Besides, they were going to throw me to Ghashiye, the giant serpent of the Underworld, or cut me in half with a saw. They wouldn't send me back to the real world, that shithole! That's why I threw caution to the wind and said rebelliously, "It's just as shitty here as it is back in the real world!"

Murnau's Faust closed his notebook and turned angrily toward me, "As punishment, you'll be sent back to that shithole!"

-9-

The table we played our nightly chess game on had been flipped over. One of the chairs had a broken leg and was lying in the middle of the floor. Everything was in disarray.

In the summer, when the weather was hot, sometimes you'd see people in the hallway shirtless. Most of the time Seyyed hung out in his room in long shorts, and he went to the bathroom dressed that way too. If anybody came to see him, man or woman, he wouldn't change what he was wearing. Very often you could also see Bénédicte without a shirt. I myself sometimes was content to wear only trousers when I was feeling lazy. But nobody ever saw Prophet shirtless. He was one of those kids from Javadiye who retained the appearances of modesty, shame, and the conservativism of South Tehran in all his mannerisms and behavior. Stranger still, in those few moments that elapsed since our arrival, both Seyyed and Prophet were in their own rooms and not a sound was to be heard suggesting any confrontation. Then, this bizarre situation . . . does that mean, Prophet had been trying to force himself on Seyyed?

When he saw me, Prophet let go of Seyyed. As he advanced, knife brandished, terror lurched within me. His huge, round eyes, which inspired fear even under normal circumstances, were so far out of their sockets they seemed pure white.

"What happened?" I asked in a hoarse voice.

"Where is he?" Prophet demanded, turning the knife on me.

Bewildered by this answer, I went to Seyyed, and this time repeated my question to him as I tried to help him up. His face pale, Seyyed gave a weak moan: "He was trying to kill me."

"Why?"

"Where is he?" Prophet asked again as he passed through the doors between Seyyed's rooms, looking around.

Having overcome some of my initial confusion and shock, when I saw Seyyed's pleading looks, I was forced to play a role that wasn't precisely within my usual repertoire. Ra'na's presence, however, and the fact that new members were continually joining the audience, lent me the strength required to perform it. So in a fatherly sort of way, I took Prophet by the arms and, trying to guide him out of the room, said, "Why did you take up a knife? So very childish!"

I was thinking we'd have achieved our goal as soon as he was out of the room; Seyyed would close the door and the ordeal would be over. But Prophet escaped my grasp with brute strength, and though I was humiliated by this, luckily he took the path I was planning on regardless. Now all we had to do was close the door and that would be it. Except, as soon as he went out of the room, he turned left and began kicking at the next door, the door to Room 4, which also belonged to Seyyed.

Now that my adrenaline had kicked in, I no longer required the external motivation of the audience to play my role, and I quickly closed the gap between us.

"Are you crazy? Why are you kicking down people's doors?"

Once again Prophet threatened me with the knife: "Where's Mehdi?"

"Who's Mehdi?

Prophet launched another kick at the door of Room 4. "Whose door is this?"

"It's the same room you just came out of," I said.

He paused. Finally, I felt like I saw my opening.

"Come and see for yourself," I immediately added in a mild tone.

Prophet came in again and passed through the doors between the rooms. As I fell in behind him, I felt a sense of victory for the first time in this dangerous game. In order to convey that feeling to Seyyed, who it seemed was just climbing up from the depths of a well, I winked at him with a satisfied smile on my face. My lashes were like two blades of shears chopping down; my wink severed Seyyed's rope when he was halfway up. It broke and he vanished back into the depths.

Maybe he supposed my bringing this monster back into the room—which he had left, after all—to be a strategic misstep. Or maybe he despaired of my idiocy since, with an ill-timed suggestion, I had revealed the existence of a door open between rooms without the landlord's permission. Especially since his arch enemy Kalantar was there, and it was possible he could cause Seyyed some trouble.

Prophet's quick retreat into the hallway showed that, despite all this, my strategy of gaining his trust had been effective. As a result, my confidence grew, and I calmly and decisively took the knife out of his hand, asking him questions about the details of what had happened all the while.

As soon as Prophet was disarmed, the dam of silence burst open. Suddenly everyone sprang into action. The hubbub grew louder as they encircled Prophet.

"What happened?"

"What's going on?" Kalantar asked Prophet, while Kalantar's wife, still distressed, asked me. Ra'na asked Seyyed.

Prophet, who saw the presence of these spectators as very fitting, abruptly climbed the ladder that always sat at the end of the hallway between his and Seyyed's rooms. Raising his hand in the air, he began his historic speech.

CHAPTER TWO

A Blurry Silver Surface

-1-

Why am I telling you all this? To change your mind?

No, it's all over for me. I know that. And I know you didn't shove your delicate hands in your coat pockets just to hide their slight trembling. I also know that the deadly flashes of light emanating from the cold metal object in your delicate hands means we've passed the point of no return.

No, I'm done for. I figured that out as soon as you showed up at my door. Such dizzying, intoxicating youth! It was like looking at my mirror image from when I was fourteen years old. The eyes were those same eyes, with deep shades of pain behind them, and the nose was that same crooked nose.

I had my doubts, as ever. Did that mean that, drowning in the fog of a time gap, I had once again set my work aside without realizing it and started doing something else, not knowing when, how, or what for? Like cigarettes, which, most of the time I lit without knowing when I'd smoked them, and I smoked without knowing when I'd put them out?

Did that mean that, suffering an episode of my chronic time gap disease, I had set my brush, pallette, and canvas aside, opened the door, turned the key in the kitchen lock, and gone straight to the mirror? Just as I was finally getting around to painting Érik François Schmidt's nose?

These are all actions that happen inside a flow of time. Let's assume it was possible this was exactly what I had done, as we sometimes do things unconsciously when doing them every day because they're so routine. What about the key to the kitchen? I always lose it in that tiny space; I put it down somewhere and forget. Or, let's suppose I'd mindlessly set my work aside and gone over to the mirror. What about my reflection? I hadn't seen my reflection in years. Not since the fateful incident.

Whenever I stand in front of the mirror, I see nothing but a blurry silver surface, empty to infinity. At first I thought there was a problem with my mirror. The terror of that day rattled my bones—the day M.A.R. came to see me while I was shaving my beard. To tell you the truth, no matter what I did, I couldn't kick the idiotic habit of shaving my beard in front of the mirror. I mean, it's true I couldn't see my reflection, but I could hear the slight sound of the razor blade scraping against my skin.

If I did shave my face, it wasn't for anyone else's benefit. The sound emanating from inside the mirror implied that my reflection was either there or should be there, but for whatever reason, it hadn't appeared on the mirror's surface yet. Like when you put a tape in the VCR and there's no picture because of a technical glitch. What if you didn't have an image but you can hear sound? What then? Wouldn't you go shave your beard in front of the mirror every day? No? You must have lost all hope, then.

Every time I shave my beard, I do it with hope. If I don't say anything to anybody about the mirror thing, it's not because I'm afraid for my reputation. You know that! They're just looking for the slightest excuse to throw you in there with the crazies, who think they're seeing all kinds of things in the desert through the hole in their cell wall, but you wouldn't see anything out there even if you stood there till Judgment Day. I shouldn't be so paranoid, you say? It just so happens that I don't see what everyone else sees when they look in the mirror. I'd have to be crazy to do something to get myself lumped in with those nutcases . . .

The first time I noticed this symptom, I acted like someone who'd just bought a VCR. I was sure the lack of a picture was a minor issue that could be resolved with a bit of tinkering, so I started experimenting with the mirror. Actually, once or twice I was able to get the reflection of the razor back for a second while I was messing around with it. Just like that, the razor was moving up and down all by itself, no hand or face in sight. Once, I was able to see its reflection for an extended period of time, so I started running tests. Or, I should say, I started seeking a logical solution to the problem, as the scientists would phrase it.

So far it had become clear that my mirror reflected objects but not people. Was this a completely logical conclusion? Not necessarily. The only thing I'd succeeded in spotting in the mirror was the razor. So I quickly got to work. First, I drew the curtains. Then, both hopeful and frightened, I picked up my toothbrush and held it up to the mirror, my heart pounding in my chest with excitement. To my complete amazement, the mirror was empty. I held the razor up again. It was there. This time I held both up together. I saw the reflection of the razor but not the toothbrush.

A bitter taste filled my mouth and I felt weak, dazed. What had happened defied all logic. I hurriedly leaned over the sink to dispose of the contents of my upset stomach, dislodged from their depths by my internal distress. It was nothing more than a couple of bitter, burning drops of bile. To rid myself of the unpleasant taste of stomach acid, I picked up my toothbrush, spread a bit of toothpaste on it and started brushing my teeth, when suddenly, my whole world turned upside down.

That night, I paraded everything I could get my hands on in front of the mirror—a skewer, the easel, shoes, a pot. In the end, I was just about ready to give up when I saw the handle of my toothbrush in the center of a ring of white foam, moving back and forth. I wanted to be sure the Theory of Objects was correct.

It was. My mirror only reflected inanimate objects. When I held up the dead cockroach that was lying under the bathroom stool, the mirror showed it. Now, what drove me to such extreme lengths was not disproving the hypothesis. I first had to establish to what extent the hypothesis was true. Even though I'd gotten positive results so far from testing hundreds of objects, one question was plaguing my mind like a thorn: "Why didn't the mirror show the toothbrush at first?"

In response to this question, I realized during repeated testing that my mirror was sensitive to my toothbrush and that, most distressingly, the only time it was reflected was when I was brushing my teeth. But more than that, what drove me to pursue the work in such a frenzy was finding the answer to this question: "Is there anything else that my mirror is sensitive to? If so, what is it?"

-2-

As Prophet climbed the ladder, I became aware of his fit, muscular body for the first time. How had I worked up the nerve to approach him like that and take the knife out of his hand? Especially considering just seeing a knife makes me break out in a sweat!

I know you're going to think I'm paranoid now. Sure, why not—I've already admitted to being afflicted with worse maladies than that. So let me tell all. In truth, I'm not willing to let a master barber shave my beard, even if you promise me Adnan Khashoggi's net worth. What guarantee is there that the barber wouldn't be struck by some sudden insanity and slice your throat from ear to ear? And what about that bib they tie around your neck, blocking off all means of defending yourself! It's true that's never happened before, not even once. But are you willing to give me a guarantee? How would you expect me to accept a guarantee like that anyway? Case in point—our very own Prophet! Who would've thought he'd go ballistic one day?

But that wasn't really what was bugging me. I couldn't believe I'd had the courage to confront Prophet, considering my fear of death. Wasn't it around that time when all those murders were happening in the streets? And a few days before that, just around the corner, some poor soul had his head cut clean off with a butcher's knife. Right under the police's nose!

Now, you're telling me, this person, whose presence in our building was suspicious from the very beginning, had lost his mind and taken up a knife? And then I, like the neighborhood tough guy, went and stood up to him? Took the knife out of his hands?

I wracked my brain to no avail, trying to figure out where such stupidity on my part had come from, especially now that Prophet had climbed up on the ladder and was saying even more terrifying things:

"The muck is rising to the ceiling, and the rotten smell of filth has enveloped everything. Indecency and degradation have surpassed all limits. This is intolerable! I have to set the record straight with everyone. I'm not gay! I'm not a fag! If anyone spreads more filth like this, I'll come after their sisters and mothers. Everyone gather here tomorrow! Men and women. I have to set the record straight with each and every one of you!"

Climbing down the ladder as quick as he'd gone up it, Prophet returned to his room. For a while, we all stared at each other in shock. Finally, Kalantar, who didn't look entirely displeased with the situation given his long-standing enmity with Seyyed, came up to me and asked, "What was the deal with that?"

I feigned ignorance, and since it was late, I suggested everyone go back to their rooms and we deal with the situation tomorrow when we were calmer. With this short speech, I was actually trying to get Kalantar and his wife off my back as soon as possible. Especially since I was afraid that if this little gathering in the hall continued on, the crisis would escalate, or someone would let something slip that caused the djinn, who had returned to the bottle of his own volition, to reemerge with a wisp of smoke.

Kalantar and his wife went back to their room. Ra'na and I went to Seyyed's room. The bells of Saint-Paul Saint-Louis Church tolled one o'clock in the morning.

-3-

I couldn't believe it. It was the worst punishment imaginable for me.

"You're joking."

"No joking here!" replied Murnau's Faust. "You'll be sent back to that shithole called the real world!"

He said it with such finality, my stomach dropped. I cursed myself inwardly for being so disrespectful to such kind beings and for piquing their anger, which resulted in a punishment the likes of which I couldn't have even imagined.

In despair, I set the last arrow in my quiver to the bow: "Look, gentlemen. I'm ill. It's not within my control. You know I have self-destructive tendencies. It was poor, late Bernard who discovered my illness. If he hadn't, even I wouldn't have known. In any case, I apologize for my offensive behavior."

"That's not the issue," said the invisible partner.

"Then what is it?"

"You've committed multiple murders!"

My head swirled. Did that mean . . . was it possible in those moments when I was suffering time gaps, I'd killed someone without knowing it? Like I was sleepwalking?

I'd been known to wash my hair dozens of times in the shower, since every time I suffered a time gap right in the middle of it, and I didn't know if I'd washed my hair or not, so I decided not to risk it and started all over again.

I'd been known to climb up and down the stairs of that six-floor building over and over, because every time I made it to the front door, I wondered whether I'd locked my door or not. And even when I finally did go back upstairs to check, then when I left the building again, I still doubted whether I had been in my right mind or in a time gap when I checked the door.

So, was it possible I'd killed someone and didn't know it?

Very shortly my mind was put at ease on this account: if I had killed someone and not realized it, surely the police would have! The fact that they'd never come after me meant that the hypothesis was invalid. At that moment, suddenly, my mind was drawn toward M.A.R. Was it possible I'd killed her? She was the only person who had gotten on my nerves that much. So much so that one day I pulled out a butcher's knife, my eyes seeing red, screaming that if she didn't leave me alone right then, I'd kill her.

Surely I didn't kill her myself. In that case the police would have investigated me. Was it possible I'd indirectly caused her death?

My chest tightened. Not only had M.A.R. never done anything bad to me, she was the only person who had ever really loved me. I'd known her for many years. Many years before I came here. In those days, I was embarking on yet another one of my dead-end careers. I was singing, and had just given a concert at the Italian embassy that had caught M.A.R.'s attention. Though we didn't know each other, she somehow got a hold of my phone number and asked to meet me.

The day she came, I was shaving my face, as usual, without being able to see myself in the mirror. I had just lathered shaving cream on my face when once again the desire seized me to experiment with the mirror. I was really getting into it when the buzzer for my apartment rang. I gave her directions to the entryway and quickly returned to the bathroom.

I didn't know what to do. I was never able to fully wake up until I'd shaved my beard. But if I shaved it, she might pop in while I was busy doing it and then I'd bungle things and my secret would be revealed. I was weighing the pros and cons when suddenly an image appeared in my mirror. Terror shivered up my spine. So the problem wasn't with my mirror!

"Don't be scared!"

Until that moment, shame had never let me look directly at her face. And now that I saw her in the mirror, I had a chance to study her face carefully for the first time. What a charming face!

The rays of a smile illuminated my mirror.

"With all this foam on your face, you look like Colonel Sanders!"

I was delighted by what she said. I don't know why, but for some reason I'd always dreamed of being a colonel. Maybe because a colonel is someone with a clear purpose. He's passed through the difficult and arduous initial stages of military training, and although he's already in a good position, he has even brighter prospects for the future ahead of him. A colonel may even have access to secrets that the ranks above and below him don't have. In the military, the lower your rank, the closer you are to death. A private who is fighting on the front lines is cheek to cheek with death, while a commander is a bit further away, depending on his rank. A colonel is so far removed from death (assuming, of course, that he hasn't died already), that he looks down on it from above. From then on, the higher the rank you attain, the further removed you become from a death in action, and the closer you get to a different kind of death—an unexpected death. A colonel stands about equidistant from both deaths.

Despite all this, she spoke of a particular colonel, not colonels in general. As I pretended to see myself in the mirror, I said, "Colonel Sanders?"

On either side of the reflection of her pretty face, two hands appeared, and I felt their weight on my shoulders at the same time.

"The one on the KFC sign."

Suddenly the room was filled with white feathers, drumsticks, and chicken breasts. As a result of this intrusion, I retreated from the front lines of my battle against death and returned to the apartment bathroom once more.

I was upset that she'd crushed my dreams of colonelhood. In that moment, I decided to do something that would force her to immediately run away. I stared directly into her eyes and said, "Do you see me in the mirror?"

"How come?"

"I don't see myself!" I confessed, like I was admitting I was a leper.

"Me neither!"

I was overjoyed by her response, and instead of asking her exactly what she meant—whether it was me she didn't see or herself—I fell in love with her.

-4-

Seyyed was looking pale. The magnetism that drew everyone toward him was temporarily out of commission. Although he rarely lost himself, in those rare instances when it did happen, I saw how that radiant complexion of his, which lent his face a cheerful look, had been replaced by a sickly pallor. Meanwhile the delicate curve of his brow, which reflected his deeply spiritual and romantic disposition, was transfigured into broken, furrowed lines. Those long, equine features of his face and neck gave way to a punctured balloon that grew ever more deflated by the moment. And this was supposed to be the secret to his mysterious charm?

He seemed to intuit my thoughts by the way I was looking at him, and suddenly started feeling some chest tightness again. Ra'na and I had to take some preliminary steps toward first aid before asking him any questions as to the events of that evening. As soon as we laid him down on the bed, Ra'na began rubbing his chest, and I went to get the phone.

It was unplugged, and the outlet had been wrenched off the wall. When I plugged it back in, Seyyed said in a weak, raspy voice, "Are you calling for me?"

"You must have the emergency medical numbers memorized by now."

"No, I'm fine. I have to go."

"Go where? In this state?" Ra'na asked.

"I have to go. Agnès will get worried."

I knew nothing bad would happen if he didn't go. To be honest, they were one of those married couples that lived their lives totally independent from one another.

"Don't you think she'll be more worried if she sees you like this?" I said. "Especially since it's late and she has to go to work early?"

"She'll be more worried if I don't come home."

"But she doesn't know, does she?"

Seyyed fished a packet of Lysanxia pills out of his pocket and said in a muffled tone, "I was talking to Agnès on the phone when that madman broke down the door and barged in."

"Why'd he do that??" I asked quietly.

Seyyed popped a few pills in his mouth at once and as he swallowed them, lowered his voice in turn: "He was holding the knife to my throat and kept asking, 'Where's Mehdi?'"

Ra'na, who was usually pretty loud, asked "Who's Mehdi?"

Worried the djinn I'd struggled so hard to put back in the bottle would reappear, I gestured to Ra'na we'd better keep quiet for the time being.

As our voices subsided, Seyyed and I stared at each other. It felt like something in the room had cracked. The tip of Prophet's blade hadn't spilled any blood, but it shattered something that was irreparable—the wall of our personal safety. Now we had to weigh every word we said and make sure we struck the right tone, relative to the risk.

Seyyed stood up and grabbed his keys. Completely drained and craving alone time to detox from the poison of this awful night, I asked him half-heartedly if he wanted me to accompany him. He said he would go alone. And alone he went. When I went back to my room, Ra'na, who would normally cancel any plans we'd made with the flimsiest of excuses, came with me.

I wanted to lie down and think about absolutely nothing, but Ra'na was sitting on the edge of the bed. I was stuck thinking about how I could get rid of her, when she leapt up without warning, like a woman who sensed her man was teetering on the water's edge again.

"His heart!" she exclaimed. "He shouldn't be left alone. If he has another episode . . ."

Without waiting for my reply, she rushed down the stairs three at a time in slippers and just a thin gown, despite the cold weather outside. I said to myself, "Our feet certainly seem to reveal all our secrets, don't they?"

-5-

The cross of the Saint-Paul Saint-Louis Church stood directly opposite my window. Its clock struck one-thirty in the morning. And I, who had thought I would finally finish the portrait of Érik François Schmidt that night, was now lying tired and anxious on my bed, bringing what little remained of that harrowing night to a close by considering several riddles that were tangled up with each other like a ball of yarn with no end. The only discernible lead was so useless that with the first tug, it came free from the rest. No matter where I began, I kept coming to the same conclusion that the key to solving this mystery was, unfortunately, that same solitary lead. I had to figure out who Mehdi was.

Of my fellow Iranians living on this floor, the only person who was absent (besides Ali, who either wasn't there that night, or was there but didn't come out of his room) was a young man named Fereydoon, whose room was directly across from mine. His neighbor to the right was Seyyed and to the left was Bénédicte.

Fereydoon and Prophet moved into this floor around the same time, thanks to Kalantar's maneuverings. With my arrival (which was orchestrated by the many efforts of Seyyed), the balance of power in the battle between Seyyed and Kalantar had temporarily shifted in favor of Seyyed. Kalantar, who had felt isolated for some time, finally saw his chance to swing the war his way, first by luring Fereydoon and Prophet to this floor, and second, by traveling home and marrying a tough, hardy woman. That's how the long hallway on our rudderless planet-ship abruptly transformed into the arena of slippers, pajamas, bowls of traditional aash-e reshte noodle soup, and debates over democracy, which took place at night in Fereydoon or Kalantar's rooms, and sometimes got heated when others joined in. Little by little, our conversations were infused with the smell of sautéed onions, laying the groundwork for future catastrophes.

Fereydoon was a polite young man I saw around more often than Prophet because our rooms were right across from each other. He was extremely kind, and whenever we ran into each other, he always offered to do something for me or help me out, especially around the house, since he was well-versed in carpentry, construction, and plumbing. It was obvious from his sturdy work clothes and specialized tools that he made his living that way. Though he had offered to help me over a hundred times, now that I actually needed him, he was nowhere to be found.

Logically, Kalantar must have known who Mehdi was. However, despite the dangers that it entailed, I preferred to ask Prophet himself rather than Kalantar, whom I considered to be responsible, in a way, for everything that had happened.

I decided to go that very evening and knock on Prophet's door for the first time. The strange events of that night notwithstanding, his nature had been an enigma for me from the very beginning. He'd never participated in the discussions of the young liberals, other than once or twice just after he arrived. He mostly stayed in his room and more often than not, other people went to see him, especially Fereydoon. I asked myself, "He doesn't work, so how does he eat? He's not the type to get all wrapped up in his thoughts, so what does he stay up all night doing?"

The only clues that allowed me to sketch a vague outline of his personality were the unpleasant sound of him clearing his throat (which he did every few minutes), the occasional sound of his wooden bed tapping against the wall (which could be an indication he had sat down or stood up), and the intermittent sound of something like a glass marble falling on the floor. Although this was an odd, unrecognizable sound, there was an even stranger sound, which you could hear a lot of the time, usually around midnight, which sounded like someone was dusting the walls with a broom. At first I thought he was painting, but when it didn't let up, I wondered, "How long could it possibly take to paint a room that's ten by ten meters?"

Now, all these bizarre, nebulous signs, combined with my unanswered questions, were whirling around in my mind like a tornado, tormenting me. I couldn't figure out why Prophet had held a knife to Seyyed's throat, who Mehdi was, or what the relationship was between these two things, but at least one thing was obvious: someone had accused Prophet of being gay. And although the relationship between this fact and the other two questions was impossible to discern, with a little bit of conjecture, you could conclude that this proud, traditional young man had flown off the handle when an unseemly accusation was made against him, and he wanted to repair his stained reputation. In that case, who had made the accusation? Seyyed? Why was he looking for Mehdi, then? Could it have been me? If so, why did he go after Seyyed?

My head pounded with a splitting headache. I thought I'd go to the kitchen and take some painkillers, but right when I stood up, a sound grabbed my attention. A door opened and a pair of slippers came from the end of the hallway toward my room. When you live in attic rooms, after a while you come to know everyone by the sound of their footsteps. It was Kalantar. The slippers passed by my door and stopped a little beyond it. There was a knock on Prophet's door.

Without meaning to, I listened in.

-6-

No, I wasn't in front of the mirror. Does that mean—was it possible that this was that same long-lost image of me at fourteen years old? For a moment, I felt that I had gone mad. But how can an insane person distinguish the line between madness and sanity? Anyone whose mental stability has been destroyed starts out on a path, and it ends in a place called insanity. But where is this place? Without a doubt, some people stop after advancing some ways down the path and, if circumstances allow, turn around and slowly go back the way they came. This place, however—this border between lucidity and lunacy, which is invisible until we've crossed it—would we be aware of it if we had traversed it? Certainly, for others the question is clear. But what about for ourselves? Haven't you seen those crazy people who warn you they're not crazy and you, all of you onlookers, laugh at them? So is it possible that I too have crossed over this line and am unconscious of it? It's true that if they posed my case to a psychologist, discounting the three so-called illnesses (that is, the time gaps, self-destructive tendencies, and the mirror illness), he would conduct himself as if he had a very serious case in front of him indeed. Despite all this, no one had called me nuts yet. But what about now? Now that someone had knocked on my door and, just as I opened it, I saw myself facing someone that looked like me, like the last image I'd seen of myself in the mirror?

I unconsciously stumbled backwards. Without saying a word, he came in, shut the door, pulled up a chair and sat right there in front of the door in complete silence, staring at me.

"You . . ." I began, unable to complete my sentence. The way he looked at me, every single question proved to be pointless before it was asked. Like a person searching for an unknown object amongst the dusty furniture of an abandoned storage closet, I rummaged through my vague, forgotten memories for an answer, though the question was still unclear to me.

I fixed my eyes on him. Something emanated into the atmosphere from his entire being, something that told me he came from my very flesh and blood, from the same raw materials as me. The occasional slight trembling of his upper lip betrayed a pain which brimmed over and could not be confined to his body. In the end, I thought I'd dispense with any kind of pointless inquiry into his identity and instead offer him something, since he looked tired and it seemed had traveled a long way: "You must be thirsty." He just stared at me. "The kitchen's on the other side of the stairwell," I said. "Let me bring you a cold soda." As I got up to go, he held up his left hand.

Involuntarily, I sat down. His right hand had been in his coat pocket the entire time. By forcing me to sit with his left hand, my attention had been drawn to his right, which was tensed up like he was squeezing something in his fist.

I might have thought that my time was up, that he was one of the innumerable agents of the Islamic Republic that turned up in every city during that time. But his silent resemblance to me made me doubt, and now, the way that he held up his left hand, and that familiar movement he'd made with his eyebrows at the same time, was like a face that slips out from behind the mask for one moment, and it jogged something in my memory. When I looked carefully, I saw that, despite his resemblance to me, there was something in him that reminded me of M.A.R. For a split second an insane thought crossed my mind—was it possible I'd gotten M.A.R. pregnant and hadn't known?

The last time I'd seen her was fifteen years ago. She relied on her body's monthly cycle and its natural feminine rhythm as a birth control measure. As in all other health matters, she didn't take any pills to deal with it. That night she told me it could be risky and asked me to come up with a solution. And I, who hadn't thought ahead about anything, retreated into my shell, disappointed and mopey, and stared at the intricate crown molding on the ceiling, searching for something vague and uncertain.

She knew it was the last night and that this might be the last time we met. When she saw how dejected I was, she wrapped her arms around my neck and pulled me into an embrace: "I hope nothing happens. But if it does, so be it!"

-7-

"I know you're awake. Open the door."

Still no answer. When Kalantar persisted for the third time, I heard Prophet's voice saying in a decisive tone, "Leave me alone!"

Kalantar went back to his room. And I realized for the first time how thin these walls were if someone was trying to listen in. All this time we thought we were totally unobserved in the privacy of our rooms, but we were actually naked in front of each other. It's true that whenever Kalantar and his wife were making love, all of us felt a little sorry for what the woman was enduring, and we couldn't focus on any particular task until her moans subsided. It's true that every time George Bizet's *Carmen* was blasting from Room 9—which was at the end of the hallway right across from Milosh—we all knew that Emmanuelle, a girl who lived on the third floor with her family, had come to avail herself of the enrichments of the operatic arts, far from the prying eyes of others with her friend, Jean. It's true that every time Prophet cleared his throat, something sharp and rough passed through the walls and scratched my eardrums. But I didn't think the voices of two people talking at a normal volume could be heard so easily. It's true that at that moment I had become intensely curious, and at other times I was too preoccupied to pay attention to what other people were saying. But if someone were on the other side of that wall, both curious and unoccupied?

I felt like someone who had just realized what he assumed was a safe, four-wall enclosure was, in fact, a stage. What he imagined to be a solid wall was really a one-way mirror with an audience on the other side.

Without meaning to, I started reconsidering everything that had happened during that time.

Except for the mirror disease, I didn't have anything in particular to hide. Nearly everyone, however, has little secrets that he will carry with him to the grave. There are also secrets that we try to hide from other people to the extent possible. Like a six-fingered person who constantly tries to hide their sixth finger.

Now I was trying to recall which one of my sixth fingers I had put on display for Prophet. Without a doubt, what had happened between me and Ra'na was not something to be proud of. Did that mean Prophet knew about everything that had transpired between us?

Prophet's bed knocked against the wall a few times and made a rapping sound.

I listened in. I heard the slight, repeated sound of something like a glass marble hitting the floor. I was waiting for something terrible to happen at any moment. But another sound that was coming from the stairwell at the same time drew me out of my perplexed state: the same footsteps that had gone rapidly down the six flights of stairs an hour ago, taking several at a time, were now coming back up, heavy and plodding.

I leapt up immediately. Considering the new developments in our situation, talking in this room was not without its dangers, even about insignificant things. Plus, I didn't want to be careless. For the past twenty days, ever since Ra'na was obliged to start sleeping in the kitchen, she would make up any excuse to come to my room. It wasn't her fault. My kitchen was a bare room with an old bed shoved into one of the corners. The greasy, beat up walls really put you off. This room, on the other hand, had a beautiful carpet which lent it a warm atmosphere, and if you got bored, there were books handy and you could listen to music. I knew all this very well, but considering our history together, there was no other way.

Ra'na's plodding, heavy footsteps were approaching. I grabbed my key and moved to the kitchen. That way, I could say goodnight whenever I wanted and retreat to my room.

-8-

No, I hadn't killed anyone. When M.A.R. came back to see me, the very act of picking up the butcher's knife had calmed me down. So, with a hint of self-righteousness, I said, "Murder? I've never so much as slapped anyone in my entire life."

"Murder, spreading misinformation, and threatening public safety." Murnau's Faust replied calmly.

I had fallen into a rushing whirlpool, and every attempt to struggle merely dragged me further under. Casting about for a piece of driftwood to cling to, I said, "Well in any case, I don't suppose you'll send me back there just like that."

I was hoping that by saying this, I'd at least get to stand trial and have the opportunity to defend myself, but the situation only deteriorated from there.

"You won't be sent back in the same form, that's for sure. A harsher punishment is in store for you, because on top of everything else you've committed another sin, which has so far been unprecedented."

"What sin?" I asked, stunned.

"Not only did you live your entire life cheating and lying—you've kept up your deceptions here!"

"What deceptions?" I replied helplessly.

Gesturing to my book, Faust said, "You knew this day would come, so you tried to get ahead of it. To mislead everyone, you wrote the record of your deeds in advance, the way you wanted, not the way things really happened."

"I'm sorry," I said. "Is this a trial, or a discussion of literary critical theory?"

"Don't think you can take advantage of our ignorance of literary matters here and derail the course of the trial!" said the invisible partner.

Faust added, "In a note you wrote in the book, you admitted that the murder occurred. You tried, however, to muddy the waters of the initial case by bringing in this, that, and the other. You wrote, 'Who is the murderer? Seyyed Alexander? The madman next door (by which you meant Prophet)? My son? Or Khatoun, who is the harbinger of death wherever she goes?'"

"I trust my own mind to discern the truth, more than what actually happens," I replied. "You know better than anyone that what people say and do is just a screen to hide what they're thinking."

"You could have been a builder," Faust said, "Stacking up bricks from morning till night, and if you'd made a mistake, the bricks would have only cracked open your own skull. But with those yarns you wove together, you ruined the lives of multiple people."

"You accused poor Seyyed, who would've gone to the ends of the earth for you, of being insane!" said the partner.

"Érik François Schmidt, poor man, was devastated when he read your book!" Faust added.

"Ra'na threw herself in front of a train out of despair!" said the invisible partner.

-9-

I woke up at 2:00 PM, as usual. I thought, once I'd washed up a bit, I'd buy a bouquet of flowers and head to the cemetery. Then I'd visit the old folks' home. When I went to turn the key in the lock of the kitchen door, it occurred to me I should knock, as I'd been doing lately. But Ra'na, who had gradually learned to recognize peoples' footsteps just like everyone else (and, I found out later, kept an eye on the hallway by watching out the keyhole), opened the door for me.

I didn't understand what this meant. By force of habit, I picked up the kettle to fill it up and put it on the stove before washing my face.

"Let's go out. Please," Ra'na said.

She was shaking. Holding the kettle under the tap, I said, "What's wrong?"

"Let's go out. I can't say here."

The night before, when she walked Seyyed to his wife's house, she didn't have anything important to say when she got back. Now what had happened in the meantime that made her insist like this?

I thought maybe during that brief window last night, she and Seyyed had exchanged some words she felt weren't appropriate to convey to me right then. To tell you the truth, I sensed something had been going on for quite a while. In such cases, incidents like what happened last night can be a decisive factor in causing secrets to come out unexpectedly. I won't hide the fact that I wasn't thrilled by this turn of events, for completely personal reasons. At the same time, I had been anticipating this day for a while, since I assumed it was inevitable. I said coolly, "Fine, wait till the tea is ready and then we'll go."

Ra'na's answer made me concerned: "Please!" she said, "Just have something at the cafe!"

She was so pale and on edge, her hands trembling, I couldn't help but imagine any number of terrible things. I was just standing there numbly when she took the kettle out of my hand, looking pathetic, and rested her arm on my back, tenderly and with a kind of hope.

"I'm begging you!" She said as she shepherded me toward the bathroom. "Splash some water on your face and let's hurry up and go."

-10-

The fact that I couldn't see myself in the mirror caused a whole host of problems, both minor and major. One of the minor problems was my face always had cuts on it because I had to shave without a mirror. Worse still, because I couldn't see the effects of time on my face, I always pictured myself with my fourteen-year-old self in mind (which always made me act childish, despite my age). The major problem was that I fell pointlessly in love with M.A.R. and laid the groundwork for my murder with my own hands.

But, this disease had one enormous plus side. It was like a lab that allowed me to conduct experiments and find out certain things I wouldn't have been able to otherwise. Very often, I was mired in despair and so mentally and physically numb, Oblomov seemed like a cheery, joyful person to me. In my eyes, nothing held any interest. No matter what I looked at, I would only notice its downsides right off the bat.

Once, an older gentleman who seemed to comprehend my pain said to me, "Try to love something. Doesn't matter what. God, a woman, music—even alcohol or opium. Just love something!"

I'd stopped singing a while ago since I couldn't give up creature comforts like smoking and drinking. Alcohol and opium are sedatives. You can take sedatives but you can't love them. So, at the same time, I tried to love someone.

Yet, even though this theory was the only treatment for people like me, like every other theory it had one critical flaw: since the thing you loved became the very anchor of your existence, it had to be, like every sought-after perfection, completely flawless. I couldn't find anyone like that. Whenever I encountered a woman who I thought might represent perfection, from the very first moment I would start scanning for flaws, just to be sure. Of course, I always found them. That's why I was constantly suffering in absolute despair, and every time I was in absolute despair, it was the mirror that saved me. Anytime I doubted whether I was alive or not, I would go to the mirror and say to myself, "See? It doesn't show your reflection. So you must not have turned into an inanimate object yet!"

My precious lab, which had saved me from misery so many times, also helped me make another important discovery later on.

For some time, one of my body parts hadn't been working properly. One day, when I was really miserable, I said to myself, "I should get help from the mirror. If it's dead, its reflection should show."

I quickly made my way to the kitchen, drew the curtain and stood in front of the mirror. The bathroom mirror wasn't big enough for my purposes. I knew enough about physics to know that I needed to move back a little to get the right angle. My kitchen, however, was a small space and new technologies still hadn't advanced enough to make it possible to push the walls back instantly like you could in a cartoon, where it was easy as pie. Another thing that made this operation more challenging than usual was that it was very difficult for me to figure out which part of my body was in front of the mirror, since I couldn't see my reflection.

In the end, keeping in mind some complex mathematical calculations, I got up on the stool and positioned myself in front of the mirror, aiming to get the right angle. Finally, in one of the most difficult and ridiculous positions, I caught a glimpse of the reflection of the sought-after member.

I plopped down glumly on the stool and stared off into a random spot in space. Psychologists and sociologists had noted that this was one of the side effects of being in exile. It was considered the primary factor in families breaking up after they'd left the home country. I knew many exiles in my circle who had experienced similar side effects, but a mysterious power told me that someone else had been the primary cause of my misfortunes.

-11-

Seyyed knew my habits well and respected them with a particular attention to detail. Most of the time he called at two o'clock sharp, or just after, to make sure I was awake. That day, too, he called when I was tying my shoelaces so we could go out with Ra'na. He wanted to see what the situation was in our building. Freaked out and no longer willing to trust those paper-thin walls, I asked if he was calling from Agnès's house. He said yes. I told him I'd call him back in a few minutes. At Café de Phares, Ra'na told me part of the story. I called him from right there in the cafe, and he joined us as soon as he could.

On the sidewalk in front of the cafe, two chubby penguins danced and sang happy, satirical lyrics to a tune from a Tex Avery cartoon. The clapping sound of their plastic feet on the cobblestone sidewalk pierced the tense, anxious atmosphere created by Ra'na's words.

She trembled the entire time she spoke. Seyyed and I stared at each other in silence. We had to come up with something. No doubt the events of last night were just the beginning and we should expect worse times ahead.

"I don't dare set foot in there again," Seyyed said.

His words plunged me into some strange, conflicting feelings. On the one hand, I was happy that the incident with Prophet had thrown some obstacles in the way of the painful course of events that had begun with Ra'na's arrival. On the other hand, it troubled me to think that our nightly chess games might be interrupted, games which had become like a drug to help me stomach the frozen time of exile.

"Maybe we should go talk to him," I said.

"What could we possibly say?" Ra'na said. "The guy's totally nuts!"

Based on what limited intel I'd gleaned from here and there, I knew Prophet had married a French woman and had a son by her, and that a year ago he'd left both of them. After a long period of drifting, he had eventually ended up in the room next door.

I said, "Anyone who holes himself up in his room day and night like that is liable to go insane. We have to see what's causing his suffering."

"What's it got to do with us?" Ra'na said.

She said it like everything that had happened was my fault. Then she added, "Are we the ones who caused his suffering? Is that why he held a knife to one of our throats and terrorized one of us all night long?"

"We should have called the police right then," Seyyed said.

"They'd have thrown him in prison or taken him to the mental hospital," I said.

"So much the better!" Ra'na spat venomously.

The Prophet incident had clearly divided us into two camps: Seyyed and Ra'na on one side, and me on the other. I saw a particular meaning in this division—it had to do with an entirely different battle that was being fought secretly. With my lenient approach to Prophet, I was deepening the divisions between our two camps, which were more at odds than ever before. It was as if I unconsciously wanted to dredge that covert battle up from the depths and force it to the surface, so it could be superimposed onto our overt conflict. That's why, every single time, my sympathy for Prophet fanned the flames of Ra'na's rage and animosity. I don't blame her, either. She spent the entire night petrified and trembling, and fatigue and lack of sleep had seriously taken a toll on her nerves. Apparently Prophet had camped outside her door all night.

It was easy to spot the difference between Prophet's footsteps and everyone else's. His feet slapped on the ground hard, and he walked so quickly, he practically sliced the air in half. That night, I also heard him passing back and forth in the hall more than usual, but I assumed he was going to the bathroom so much because he was tormented by guilt. At one point when I was going to the bathroom, I did see him on the landing of the stairwell. He was standing right on the other side of my kitchen wall. At first, I was a little surprised. Then, I thought maybe he needed Kalantar for something, had knocked on the door, and now was waiting off to one side out of embarrassment. I did grow a little concerned when he kept going back and forth all night, but to tell you the truth, I wasn't about to go asking any questions.

Now Ra'na was saying that the first time Prophet passed by, he pounded on the kitchen door. Then, pacing in the hall all night until morning, he'd rap on the door once every few minutes, scaring Ra'na out of her wits every time.

"Why didn't you tell me?" I said.

"I was afraid if I made a sound," she replied, "he'd break down the door and do to me what he couldn't do to Seyyed."

As I listened to all this in total shock, I wanted to believe that divine punishment was real.

Now, in this mysterious silence that had drawn a halo around our table and separated it, like a ship adrift, from the atmosphere of the rest of Café de Phares, each of us was thinking in some way about the future. A future that we were for sure all envisioning differently. And since I was only thinking about the future of our chess matches, I said, throwing an anchor overboard for our drifting vessel, “Maybe it’s better if we bring the matter up to Érik François Schmidt.”

“Schmidt can’t do shit!” Seyyed said, waving his arm in the air,

“He gave that room to Prophet temporarily,” I said. “If he finds out about what happened, maybe we’ll be free of Prophet sooner rather than later.”

“If Érik François Schmidt were capable of doing anything, the building wouldn’t be the way it is!”

He was right. In this city where every building had a proper door and padlock, the door to our building was always open. Not only did it not have a lock, it wouldn’t even latch shut. In winter, the stairwell was overrun by so many homeless people and roving drunks, whoever needed to come upstairs at night had to pick his every foothold carefully, like a mountain climber, lest he kick someone. And kind, sensitive Érik François Schmidt saw all this and didn’t get upset. He may have even felt a deep satisfaction in his heart of hearts.

The chubby penguins, which looked strangely alike, were now weaving in and out of the customers and collecting money.

A mysterious force called me back to my room. I jumped out of my seat.

Seyyed was stunned: “Where to?”

“I just remembered I have something important to do!”

-12-

We hadn't heard the sound of *Carmen* coming from Emmanuelle's room for a few days. I thought they'd probably gone out, but an hour ago I saw her friend, Jean, coming out of the bathroom. As soon as he saw me, he slinked through the door into the room, nervously, like a cat.

There was no sign of Ali's amateur prayer sessions or the unnerving moans of Kalantar's wife. If not for the occasional mild reverberation of Milosh's cello, I would have thought Bénédicte was making a scene again, since, as I came in, I happened to notice the latest issue of the newsletter for our rudderless planet-ship on the wall: "TRASH BAGS **DO NOT** BELONG IN THE HALL. ANYBODY WHO CAN'T UNDERSTAND THIS BETTER FUCK OFF SOMEWHERE ELSE AND GET LOST!"

I didn't put my trash bags in the hallway, but I still came to the conclusion that I better fuck off somewhere else and get lost. Even prior to recent events, Bénédicte's behavior had gradually been deteriorating into unbearable torture. I was quite possibly the only person who hadn't fallen for her nonsense yet, only because I avoided interacting with her as much as possible. Whenever I wanted to leave my room, I stood there and listened first. If she was in the hallway, I waited until she went back to her room. I mean, she scared the crap out of me right from the very beginning. My first or second night in the building, I came out around dawn to go to the kitchen. Since the hallway light switch was on the other side of Bénédicte's door, I had to traverse a short distance in the dark before reaching it. In front of Bénédicte's door, my foot caught on a body. In terror, I yelped and turned on the light. A drunk man lying in front of Bénédicte's door opened his red, puffy eyes for a moment and looked at me.

From then on I was careful at night. Around midnight, the drunk would come and knock on Bénédicte's door: "Please, Bénédicte . . ."

Bénédicte never answered. He would lay down in front of the door. Every once in a while he woke up and knocked again: "It's cold, Bénédicte. Please, I'm begging you."

When the sound of his knocking grew loud, Bénédicte opened the door violently and said, "Get lost, asshole! I put up with you for all those years."

Then came the sound of cursing, kicking, and something like a sack of potatoes falling down the stairs.

A few months later the drunk vanished forever, but Bénédicte's little disruptions weren't going anywhere. The only difference was now the type of disturbance was always unpredictable. Sometimes at four in the morning, she'd scream and pound on the neighbor's door to her left or right and raise hell. I'd been awake and heard nothing, but she, who'd been asleep and was a heavy sleeper too, claimed a noise had woken her up.

Sometime after the drunk man disappeared, Bénédicte decided to start publishing her wall newsletter in the bathroom. "PLEASE CLEAN THE TOILET AFTER USE." The first few issues of her newsletter didn't gain much traction, so the tone gradually became more aggressive: "WHOEVER STILL DOESN'T KNOW HOW TO USE THE TOILET IS GOING TO EAT SHIT IF HE SETS FOOT IN HERE!"

The insulting messages in the bathroom were getting on everyone's nerves, but to be fair, the mess in there had become an issue for us as well. Everyone asked each other who could be doing it. They all claimed that not only did they clean it, they disinfected it once or twice a day. Everyone was telling the truth, too. As a result, the very existence of these writings was a mystery. Though everyone assumed Bénédicte had written them, they were all in different handwriting.

One day, Bénédicte grabbed Seyyed by the collar as he left my room, saying, "When you take a shit, clean it up, you privileged dick!"

All the color drained from Seyyed's face and he was stunned into silence. The poor guy used the bathroom on our floor as little as possible, and he was of such a refined nature that when he needed to go, he went and did his business in a cafe. I, who was of no such refined nature, of course neither went to a cafe nor complained. Very simply, I cleaned the toilet both before and after using it.

For one or two weeks in the summer, it turned out Bénédicte and I were the only ones left on the floor. And yet, the mystery remained unsolved.

One day, I woke up and went to the bathroom. When I opened the door, I wanted to throw up. For one second it crossed my mind to turn around and live that day like the refined Seyyed. But I needed to stay at home.

I picked up the brush and went at the toilet. The whole time, a question was pricking my brain like a thorn: Now that it's just me and Bénédicte on this floor, that means . . .

After the toilet was clean, I shut the door and sat down on the seat when a note on the door caught my eye, "I WANT TO TAKE THAT LAZY DOUCHEBAG WHO GAVE US THIS MASTERPIECE AND FORCE HIM TO LICK THIS PLACE CLEAN!"

Can you imagine? For one second I thought to myself, 'Don't tell me it was Bénédicte all along and now . . . now here she is thinking I'm the one who needs to make it up to her?' I came out of the bathroom, terrified. I had to steel myself for the fallout.

Last time I wasn't careful, I paid dearly for it. She left her trash bag in the hallway for three days and never took it downstairs, even though she went out every day. I had no doubt she was doing it intentionally, anticipating that I wouldn't say anything. On the fourth day when I saw she still hadn't taken it out, I was pissed. I dug up one of the old issues of the newsletter dedicated to that very topic, and I decided to tape it to her door. But I quickly changed my mind: was I asking for trouble?

I still had two or three hours left before Bénédicte would get home from work at five o'clock. I had to retreat from the precipice of disaster somehow to survive.

At five-thirty there was a knock on my door: "Are you the one who took my trash bag out?"

I thought I'd acted logically for the first time in my life, but I hadn't anticipated this turn of events. If I said yes, she might claim there was gold in it, and if I said no . . .

A thought flashed through my mind.

With total confidence I asked, "What bag?"

"Someone took my trash bag out."

"No idea."

She stood stock-still for a few moments, as if she'd been electrocuted. Then, confused and stunned, she hung her head and left. Now she was going to be racking her brain for hours trying to figure out what happened to her trash bag!

Bénédicte left, but the next day, she left her trash bag in the hall instead of taking it downstairs. If it just had a bit of chalk and some woodchips in it, it wouldn't have any smell. These bags, however, were full of garbage in the true meaning of the word. Her cat, which had been loose in the hall all day, had torn the bags open too, and a fetid stench filled the air. I knew she was waiting for me to say something.

It was no use. I either had to put up with the rotting smell in that hot weather or . . .

For one week I played the part of Madame Bénédicte's garbage man until she had mercy on me and things went back to normal. And now that the toilet incident had happened, I had to be vigilant and tread carefully.

Around dusk I was struck by an idea—I would take some of Bénédicte's old newsletter issues with me to the toilet to make sure it was really in her handwriting. When I went into the bathroom, I was stunned. The previous issue had disappeared and in its place was red writing on the door: "THESE SHITS SHOULD BE LICKED CLEAN BY WHATEVER IMBECILE KEEPS WRITING THIS NONSENSE ALL OVER THE WALLS!"

We were in the throes of madness now. There was no one in the building except for me and Bénédicte, and yet . . .

I pulled Bénédicte's old newsletter out of my pocket and compared it to the writing on the door. It was Bénédicte's handwriting! Thank God, I'd been exonerated. But that feeling didn't last: So what if Bénédicte wrote this one? Who wrote the other one then?

I shrugged and left the bathroom. Bénédicte suddenly appeared before me in the middle of the hallway, like the angel of death herself: "Did you see what they wrote on the bathroom door?"

I stared at her, stunned. No matter how I tried, I couldn't figure out where she was going with this. At a loss, I said, "Yes, I saw."

"And you didn't clean it up?"

John Cassavetes could probably handle her. I immediately slipped into character and said, "Well, it's the bathroom door, not mine!"

"Doesn't it bother you that they're writing this shit?"

Okay, now that she was ascribing the graffiti to a third person,

I could badmouth them all I wanted and they wouldn't be able to talk back. With the patient attitude of a staunch liberal, I said, "If someone feels like expressing themselves in the bathroom, what's it to me?"

The tough facade Bénédicte had been keeping up suddenly began to show some cracks. Her usually fierce glare and savage claws morphed into annoyance that subtly revealed she wasn't as strong as she seemed: "Why do I always have to clean the dumbass graffiti on the bathroom walls?"

I pitied her. In a calm tone, I replied: "I only know how to clean up other people's shit, which I am doing every day!"

After leaving Seyyed and Ra'na in Café de Phares and returning to my room, a peculiar urge struck me to go knock on Prophet's door. When the sound of Milosh's cello swelled again, I thought the moment had arrived to go and do it. The more I thought about what had happened over the past month, the more convinced I became there was a connection between Prophet's attack on Seyyed the night before and whatever was going on with me and Ra'na. Especially because after Seyyed, Prophet had gone after Ra'na. Plus, he, Ra'na and Seyyed all woke up a few hours earlier in the morning than I did. Now I was thinking, since the walls were so thin, not only was he aware of everything that happened between me and Ra'na, he probably knew lots of things I didn't!

I stood up, but at that exact moment the telephone rang. I thought it was Seyyed, but it was a long-distance call.

"Mehdi!"

"Who are you looking for?"

"Mehdi."

The snake-like rings of the telephone cord quickly uncoiled and let off a spark. My voice on the verge of breaking, I said, "Mehdi?"

"You might know him as Taqi."

Taqi lived in my place until about a year ago. Then he gave me his room and left. I knew he'd been involved in some shady things, but I didn't know he had an alias, or that it was Mehdi, of all things.

"He's gone to America," I said.

"I'm calling from America!"

"He hasn't lived here for a year."

"So that means . . ."

The silence that descended on the phone line was not of the normal variety. The voice on the other end barely managed to squeak out: "Apologies for disturbing you."

"Not at all."

With a vague nervous feeling, I stared off into space. It seemed like the person on the other end of the line was also spacing out, so they didn't hang up.

"Is something wrong?" I asked.

"So it's true!"

"What is?"

Bursting into sobs, they hung up.

-13-

There really was no solution to the problem with me and Ra'na. According to sociologists, it was one of the general experiences of exile. Every exile needs a foothold to find some purchase in their new country. They don't even get to choose where they're going to go. They have to figure out how they can leverage their foothold—which is usually a brother, sister, friend, close acquaintance, or, for those who really have no leg to stand on, sometimes the friend of a friend of a distant acquaintance. Then, they lie there, broken, on top of their host, and after a short time, the foothold is destroyed forever in accordance with the unwritten rules of exile, until they can serve as a base for the next newcomer, and the cycle repeats itself. It's nobody's fault. Neither host nor newcomer is where they belong. The host, feeling frozen in time, considers themselves a lost cause and is cold to the new arrival. Once the newcomer arrives, the host has to run around with them all over the place every day until they can find themselves a stable situation. Meanwhile, the exile finds themselves in completely the opposite emotional state. Not only are they as yet unaware of the pain of immigration, everything they look at gives off the sweet scent of freedom. The host is always living with their past, while the new exile tries to forget their past. Their conversations resemble the exchanges between a mute person lost in a dream and a deaf listener. The house is cramped, too, and they are always on top of each other. Then, they start laying into one another. Soon both have had enough, and the newcomer, irritated, has to pack their bags and go somewhere else.

But Ra'na didn't pack her bags. When I'd had enough I said, "Before that room was my kitchen, it belonged to a girl just like you for a number of years. I'll just imagine she never left. She never bugged me, so you shouldn't either!"

The problem with me and Ra'na, though, was a particular kind of problem—one that didn't have much to do with what the sociologists were talking about.

Last year, when she came here for a short visit, I acted on that older gentleman's advice to just love something. Ra'na was in love with somebody else, though, and had to go back. Ever searching for imperfections, I was afforded by her short visit a chance to infer that she had three distinct personalities. The first was a beautiful, smart woman, cheery and social, and that was the personality of hers that I fell in love with. The second was a spoiled little brat of a boy, and the third was an incredibly weak, fragile girl who temporarily gained confidence from the loving attentions of a man, but, afraid of losing them again, would claw the other person's eyes out as soon as she sensed the slightest friction.

Now that she'd come to stay, she was really a refugee of love, not politics. Her wings were wounded, and she needed time to forget the past. She needed someone to love her with his entire being and provide her the prospect of a calm and steady life.

Neither my tiny room nor my humble lifestyle provided her with such prospects, and my volatile personality didn't help. In reality, if she had three personalities, then I had an unlimited number. I was a shadow with no independent existence, so I always had to try to take on the personality of someone else. The range of choices was infinite. Sometimes I was Max von Sydow, sometimes Gérard Philipe, sometimes Jean-Paul Sartre, sometimes Dostoyevsky, and sometimes John Cassavetes. There was no keeping track of it all. I was mercurial, and sometimes I even took on the form of the person I was speaking to. Once they were totally confused, I would burst out laughing and they didn't know why, which pissed them off. Now imagine for those ten days that Ra'na and I were together, who was falling for whom!

Even worse, every time we slept together, I asked myself, "What if she's actually making love to one of my other personalities, like Cassavetes or Max von Sydow, and not me?" And she would ask herself, "What if I'm sleeping with him because of the opportunities he's given me and not because of my own personal attraction to him?" This last sentiment she expressed on the night she ended up in Seyyed's room. That night, I was at the end of my rope. Whether because of the heat or something else, I left my door open and heard her say it. At that moment I immediately realized why she decided to stop sleeping with me.

Although I was a little hurt by her decision, I wasn't really that upset: "It's no big deal, now you'll get to go back to your usual routine!"

But it seemed my usual routine was to never have one. Everything went on in such a strange way, I had no choice but to return to the kitchen with a spare key one day and tell her, with the utmost delicacy, "To me, nothing is more important than my solitude!"

The day I gave her the key, I assured her she could stay with me while she was dealing with her housing situation, as long as she didn't encroach on my independence. But still she'd come looking for me with the slightest excuse. Sometimes she wanted to go to the movies. Other times she wanted to go out to a restaurant. Sometimes right in the middle of my work, she wanted to go sit in a terrace cafe. It was an odd game. Maybe she thought her being exiled to the kitchen was a ploy on my part to get her to submit. Who knows, she might have been right! Maybe she was worried that if our relationship went south, I'd stop trying to help her find housing. But she was wrong. Not only did I follow up, I tried to entertain her as much as I could when she was bored. But how much could I really do?

So Ra'na came up with a new solution. Whenever I was in a bad mood, she went to Seyyed. Seyyed, who of course was kind, well-mannered, and good-looking.

Little by little I became convinced I was making my way out of this impasse, but Ra'na didn't change her behavior toward me one bit. She kept up her irrational expectations, which didn't fit with our new situation at all, and at the same time, she never held back in pointing out things she considered inappropriate. Whether in the kitchen or the other room, wherever she went, it was with a scornful pair of eyes that constantly kept me under scrutiny:

"Why don't you hang the key on that hook so you don't have to go searching all over for it every time?"

"Why do you shave your beard like that?"

"Why do you tie your shoelaces like that?"

"Why do you hold your knife and fork with the wrong hands?" (Why, by the way, couldn't she imagine that some people happen to be left-handed in certain instances?)

Now I understood why Érik François Schmidt never dared to throw out the young addict couple, the building's supers, who had never once cleaned the stairwell over the years, and, it was rumored, dealt drugs. Every time, in response to tenants' complaints, he resolved to be rid of them, but he immediately thought of their innocent little girl, and handled the situation by giving them a little warning.

Now, when I reflected upon the long list of countries that had been toiling for independence, in some cases for centuries, I realized why losing independence was so easy and obtaining it so difficult. I'd left my country because people were always interfering in my business, but now felt I was doomed to end up somewhere people meddled in my affairs, even after I was dead and buried.

-14-

I was utterly perplexed. The angels of death told me that after reading my book, Érik François Schmidt died from grief, even though I had just seen him today. They said Ra'na threw herself in front of a train, but she was talking to me on the phone an hour before I met my maker. What's more, my book had never been published. After the publishers told me the book was a rambling mess, I threw it in a corner and didn't even know where it was. Until that day . . .

In a smug tone I said, "My book has never been published!"

Exasperated, Murnau's Faust turned away: "I'm tired. You make him understand!"

Faust disappeared and a tall Native American appeared in his place, the one from *One Flew Over the Cuckoo's Nest.* He was standing in the exact spot Faust had just vacated. The slanted light, which hadn't budged in all that time, illuminated the right side of his face.

Fear gripped me. In a different time and place, I had learned from similar proceedings that such tactical changes meant the carrot strategy was over, and now it was time for the stick. But contrary to my expectation, it turned out the Native American's manner was extremely mild: "In your country, just like in Austria, a good writer is a dead one. Your book's not only been published—it's being widely distributed."

As soon as I heard his voice, I realized he was the invisible partner. I have to admit—his face bore absolutely no resemblance to what I had imagined. Despite all this, what he was saying about my book came as a greater shock to me.

"Even in the most advanced countries in the world, they can't publish a book that fast!" I said in disbelief.

"What do you mean 'that fast?'"

"Well, I've just joined the ranks of the departed today!"

"Everything that happens here is entirely outside of time."

"You mean I've been dead for a while?"

"Words like 'today,' 'yesterday,' and 'tomorrow' belong to that place. What time do you feel like it is right now? Day? Night? You're just dead, that's it!"

Now I understood why the slanted light never moved.

"Did Ra'na really throw herself under a train?"

"According to time here, yes. But according to time over there, right now she's sitting beside some Dutch giant, slurping up the last sip of Coca-Cola in her glass through a straw. A few minutes from now the giant will go to buy cigarettes, and Ra'na will suggest they buy your book from the local bookstore, if they have the French translation in stock. By the end of the night, Ra'na will get a hold of your book."

"And my book will be the cause of her death?"

"It made her feel hopeless. And all that time you spent falsely playing the victim made her feel guilty. Especially once you became famous after being martyred in that ghastly way. You know how your fellow countrymen are!"

At the beginning of these discussions, I'd felt a marked unease, particularly since they'd skipped over everything and jumped right to that damn book. Now that the term 'martyr' had been used with respect to me, I felt a bit calmer. I said, "And you think Ra'na has the right of it?"

"She's the one responsible for her own actions."

"It's because of her you want to send me back?"

"No one gets sent back for involuntary manslaughter."

"So why are you sending me back?"

"For opposition."

I remembered reading in the Hadith scriptures:

> On the Day of Judgment, some people will have deeds ascribed to their records that they did not commit and are not even familiar with. And when they inquire, it is said in response to them: 'You went along with a group who did these deeds and offered no opposition.'

Stunned, I asked, "Am I being sent back for opposition, or lack thereof?"

"You're being sent back for opposition."

"Opposition to whom?"

"To yourself!"

-15-

The history of the invention of the modern Iranian woman is not entirely dissimilar to the history of the invention of the automobile. The difference is that the automobile was a carriage, the content of which changed first (meaning that its horses were taken away and replaced with a motor) and then, little by little, its form shifted to be more in line with this content. In the case of the modern Iranian woman, however, the form changed first, and only then did it seek out more appropriate content. This is where the issues began to arise. (The invention of the traditional woman, which later happened in the same way, encountered no less difficulty.) This was how everyone, according to their prospects and personal taste, welded the traditional woman's mindset and the modern woman's demands together to create a composite image, which ranged in scope from the headscarf to the miniskirt. She wanted to be a party to all decisions, but all responsibilities should lie with her man. She wanted to flaunt her personality in front of others, not her sexuality, but she paraded her feminine charms around. She wore a miniskirt to put her legs on display, but should anyone say anything to her, she complained how shameless people are. She demanded to be an equal partner with the man in domestic affairs, but at the same time, considered a man who capitulates to true partnership to be weak and spineless. She wanted to weigh in on important matters, but made no effort to acquire a serious opinion. She was unhappy in her marital life but lacked the nerve to split up or cheat. She believed in gender equality and mutual satisfaction, but when it came to getting divorced, she lamented her youth that she wasted on another.

Without a doubt there were women who fell on one extreme or the other of this bell curve. But Ra'na stood right in the middle. The seventeenth night of her stay, exactly one week after our split . . . never mind. What purpose does it serve, saying these things?

I opened the door. Ra'na was sitting on the bed writing a letter. Reaching for the kettle, I saw that she'd made tea for the first time ever. I stared at her in shock. She was about to smile, and I quickly turned away and turned on the faucet. My head ached, and I felt utterly run down. I'd spent all night last night walking in the rain, cursing myself with every swear word in the book.

I looked at the mirror. Had I been able to see my reflection, no doubt my whole face would have been swollen. I washed my face and hands and tossed my lunch, which was two pieces of steak, in the frying pan. Then I started prepping a salad. I was silent the whole time as I tried to keep the mask of calm on my face. Ra'na, who was a shrewd old hand in these situations, was trying to diffuse the vibrating tension which infused the atmosphere with anxiety like a ticking time bomb. She started asking me boring questions, like how much stamps cost in other countries. I—who was on board with this effort for the time being—gave her short answers, but avoided making eye contact.

For the first time, I felt like she'd pulled herself together. The way she looked at me, which used to bug me so much, had changed. It was like she was seeing me for the first time. I'll admit, I felt pleased.

Ra'na was playing coy: "Are you thinking about something?"

"It's nothing."

"Are you upset?"

Upset? If you were in my place, you'd have ripped her head off. The night before, the seventeenth night of her stay and exactly one week after our split, I was working on my portrait of Bernard, a friend who was one of the May '68 revolutionaries. After it all went sideways, he holed himself up in his apartment for two years. When he finally came out, he headed straight for the East and spent a few years in India and Iran. He'd been making his living off introducing people to Eastern music ever since.

I was quite on edge; so much so that I kept painting and repainting the portrait. No matter what I did, I couldn't get Bernard's yawn to come out right—a yawn that wasn't the natural movement of a body, but the sudden tremor of a spirit.

This yawn happened one night when Bernard came to see me with his friend, Ingrid.

Ingrid stood next to me and rambled on the entire time I was cooking. After dinner, Bernard asked me to sing so Ingrid, who was an expert in Baroque and medieval music, could accompany me on the oboe in an improvisation.

I'd given up singing years ago, and only hummed for myself on occasion, usually while I was painting. Such was my ill luck that, one night, Bernard asked me something about Iranian music and, unable to explain it to him any other way, I was forced to sing a few bars for him. Once Bernard had heard my voice, he wouldn't let it go, especially since someone else was there who knew about my former career and had let the cat out of the bag.

Now he'd brought his friend Ingrid over so we could play something together if the opportunity arose. After dinner, we improvised a short piece. Once it was over, they encouraged and badgered me so much that I had to give in. Then when Ingrid abruptly got up to leave, she asked me to walk her out to her car instead of Bernard. Really taken aback by this suggestion, I started to laugh, "I think one of these days we've got to go looking for a place we can duel it out." As he looked at me, Bernard let out a yawn that shook his whole body.

Now, no matter what I did, I couldn't render this yawn on the canvas, which was a turning point in my relationship with Bernard and, I felt, the key to understanding what made him tick. It was nine thirty at night and my teeth were killing me, but I'd resolved to keep working, even if it took all night, when Ra'na knocked and came in.

I knew she was bored and Seyyed wasn't there to calm her down. I thought when she saw I was busy, she'd content herself with my silent company; she'd either pick up a book or keep herself entertained. So I went back to my work. She stretched out on the bed and put her well-sculpted thighs on display. I tried to regain my focus, but her accusing stare weighed on me. I knew she was about to open her mouth and scold me. She'd once said, "Why do you always paint portraits?" Another time she really let me have it: "Why do you waste so much time painting these things that nobody looks at or buys?"

In the ancient myths, an enchanting zebra always appeared before a person and led them astray. Then it would lay waste to their life so mercilessly even the non-believers pitied the humans of the mythical world, and thanked God from the bottom of their hearts that they lived in the real world. Now the enchanting zebra had reappeared, this time in the real world, and come straight to my room.

"How can you sleep with that paint smell?"

Slowly I was coming to believe that destiny was indeed a triangular thing. I had fled my father's house because a pair of critical eyes was always watching me. In Tehran, right when I went to shake those terrifying weights off my back, that other pair of accusing eyes—the Islamic Republic—came to power. And now here, just when I was catching my breath, Ra'na showed up.

"Where's the packet of painkillers I gave you last night?" I asked.

"Shall we go to the movies?" she said.

There was no longer any doubt that Ra'na had discovered my secret and realized I was nothing more than a shadow. All the same, I thought she just hadn't heard.

"My teeth hurt," I said.

"I heard *Delicatessen* is good."

All throughout history, our martyr complex and penchant for playing the victim (a peculiarly Iranian sensibility) had never allowed us Iranians to deal with our problems in good time, when they might still be solved with a slap. We let situations devolve to the point they couldn't be rectified, even with killing. Only then would we boil over, set everything on fire, and solve precisely nothing. In that moment, I embodied our history in all its meaning and picked up the paper like a long-suffering martyr, scanning the movie listings: "It's almost ten o'clock. There's a theater around here; if we hurry we can make it to the last showing."

Delicatessen was a French film, and although Ra'na had a good command of English, she knew nothing of French. The moment the film started, she turned to me angrily and said, "This film is in French!"

At that moment, the long-suffering martyr remembered his role in history. He hadn't solved things in good time with a small slap, so now it had come to this. He got up and quickly left the movie theater.

I walked around all night. In the rain. Now she was asking if I was upset?

Yes, if I was in your place, dear reader, I would have wanted to rip her head off, too. I was still planning on it, but I had to wait a bit. I said, "I have to head out soon to go to the retirement home."

"Why are you leaving?" asked Ra'na. "You're . . ."

I looked at her. She hung her head.

We were almost done eating lunch. The entire time, I tried to settle the atmosphere with small pleasantries that had a touch of kindness about them, so at least she'd be able to swallow her food.

Milosh's cello was painting dark, menacing clouds of sound that quickly moved through the sky.

Once she'd finished her cup of tea, it was time to bring the chicken I'd long fed and nurtured to the slaughter. Standing up and looking her directly in the eye, I said with a calm but firm tone, "You have one week to find somewhere else to live!"

-16-

The overcrowded, dusty room that was once full of broken, useless things was now clean and empty. On the left side of the room, up against the wall we shared, was an old wooden bed, which looked like it was turn of the century. (Who knows, maybe once upon a time it was Jean Jaurés's bed, which young Érik François Schmidt Jr. brought home as a historical souvenir from the party leader when they were getting rid of it. And then when it got rickety, he moved it to storage, since he couldn't bring himself to throw out the historical memento of the party leader, nor to see that the party leader's bed had gone rickety.)

The entire left wall, floor to ceiling, was covered with flames. Between the blazes stretching up toward heaven was an eye that had popped out of its socket, in fear of being punished. The bright red colors and the art naïf style were reminiscent of the paintings the traditional storytellers would use to spin their yarns and conjure scenes of Judgment Day, the giant Ghashiye serpent, or divine punishment. Having watched the scenes many times as a child, I wept every time for the poor martyrs who were murdered by villains, and at the end, I felt relieved when evil Harmale (who to some degree resembled our neighborhood butcher, with his bald head and handlebar mustache) was sliced in half from head to navel by the strike of the Imam's sword. Especially when I saw that in the afterlife, they boiled him in a pot and the Ghashiye serpent would eat his brains.

Oblivious to my unexpected presence, Prophet picked up a baby starling from inside a small wicker basket by the window and was petting it tenderly. At the same time, he deftly pulled sunflower seeds out of a packet on the table, cracked them, and held his mouth up to the bird's beak, holding the seed between his teeth.

I'd had plenty of reason to come, since the call from America had already cast a spark on the powder keg. So I got up and knocked on his door, not thinking about the consequences or feeling any fear of the creature who had caused such terror the night before.

Just a few minutes earlier, Kalantar had come for the second time, but as soon as he'd identified himself, Prophet once again said, "Leave me alone." And that's what provoked me even more.

When I came over, I had no plan in mind or any idea where to begin.

On the table, next to the pack of sunflower seeds, there was a book I knew well, and I felt like this was the best excuse to make my way toward the real subject. Even still, I preferred to start elsewhere, "Seems like you like taking care of birds."

"He fell out of his nest. I was afraid the dogs would tear him apart."

"Strange!" I said, supposing he'd ask, "What is?"

But he just said, "Yes, it is strange."

This exchange brought to mind the short, cryptic conversation between Ibn 'Arabi and Averroes, and I realized that I wouldn't get anywhere this way. So I occupied myself with looking at the walls.

"Did you do this painting?"

"Yes, I'm burning in the fires of hell."

Suddenly I felt really bad for this young, thirty-something man who had evoked such terror and hatred the night before. I was certain the flames that blazed up the wall of his room were sparked in the depths of his heart. I could imagine the day he came home and suddenly walked in on the woman he loved so much, whose name could have been Isabelle, or Christine, or Catherine, sleeping naked next to a young blond man, and then, instead of whipping out his knife, cutting off her head and avoiding the burning flames of hell, he did nothing and left everything up to God's judgement; because God here wasn't the same God as in Javadiyye or Darvazeh-Doulab, and only she knew if that one-year-old child belonged to him or the blond-haired man, whose name could have been Didier, Philippe, or Marcel.

"Seems like you've been working on painting it for a while?"

"How so?"

"I always hear you doing it."

"Really? Does it bother you?"

"No, I was just curious. I didn't know you were a painter, too."

"I painted it recently."

"But I've been hearing the sounds for a while. At first I thought you were dusting your wall."

"I paint over the old ones."

The time had come for me to bring up the book, which was the only book in his room. Its presence raised more questions than anything else.

"Looks like you were reading The Book of Revelations while you were doing this painting."

"I'm always reading it."

"I thought you were religious, but it seems like you've converted."

He reached under the table and pulled out another book from a place I couldn't see. "I'm a monotheist. The only books I read are the Torah and the Quran."

A snake coiled around my heart. I suddenly remembered the discussions I'd had with Seyyed and Ra'na just hours before in Café de Phares. Seyyed said, "I couldn't believe how athletic and strong he was."

"His sudden movements catch you off guard, like someone who does karate," I said.

"Did you see the tags hanging around his neck?" Ra'na asked. "They looked like dog tags!"

The hand of God had begun appearing, both here and at home, for a while now. It reached out from under the sleeves of Men of God from time to time to cut militant infidels' heads off. I, who had left my father's house and escaped to Tehran out of fear of those hands, went one step further and left my country when they came to power, fleeing here. But now I was realizing those hands were directly in front of me. In the room right next to mine!

CHAPTER THREE

A Presence of the Talking Kind

-1-

Why doesn't he say anything? Why won't he let me offer him anything? Why is he so upset? His black pants are dusty. His face is dusty. His shoes are covered in dirt. Where did he come from?

It's not like this is a desert. Everything's paved around here. So where'd he come from? If he's really my flesh and blood, why didn't M.A.R. say anything? She was here just the other day. After fifteen years! I hope this isn't what she came to say.

I stand up to turn on the light. He leaps up so quickly, I instinctively stop. Despite my age I feel like a kid in front of him. For one second, I want to throw myself at his feet, but a force emanates from him that pins me to the spot. There's a kind of magnetism radiating off his being as he sits there. Something that forces me to sit respectfully. But the room is getting dark. In a few minutes, how will I be able to see him without turning on the light? He says nothing. His clothes are dark too. In total darkness . . . if that hand . . .

Why is he hiding his right hand in his pocket? In total darkness . . . then I'll just have to speak. Speak so I'm not afraid. Speak so I don't feel anything. Not a thing. Not the movement of a hand, not the slice of a sharp blade. I have to keep on talking. Like those times when I'd go walking in the desert at night, all alone. I sang so I wouldn't be afraid. I sang so if a djinn blocked my way, I could imagine I was blazing a path with my voice. Now I have to speak. He knows once it gets dark, he won't be able to contain me with his gaze anymore. Once it gets dark, his presence will have to be a presence of the talking kind. Once it gets dark, he too will have to become someone else. I know that when it gets dark, I too will fade to black.

-2-

The phone was ringing. I opened my eyes. It was two in the afternoon. I knew it was Seyyed. He wanted to check if I was alive or not. I was alive.

The day before, when I'd gone to see Prophet, I heard my phone ringing from his place, once every few minutes. I knew right away it was Seyyed, who was worried about me. When I came back from Prophet's, the phone rang again as soon as I opened the door. I picked up the receiver. Ra'na was on the line. She said she and Seyyed had been taking turns calling me for the last hour. I told her there was no need to worry.

"I wanted to come back," she said, "but I didn't dare come up the stairwell on my own. Come to the door if you can. I'm afraid that maniac will show up again."

I asked where they were; she said the usual cafe. I told them to wait until I got there. Half an hour later, after they'd heard the details of my meeting with Prophet, our table once again seemed to be drifting apart from all the other tables at Café de Phares, like a ship without an anchor.

The phone was still ringing. Lying in bed, I yawned and picked up: "Are you here?"

"Yes, I'm here."

"I'll be there in a few minutes."

Ever since the night of the incident, Seyyed's voice had become thin and raspy. He wouldn't risk coming to this floor alone anymore. Now that he was sure I was in my room, he wanted to come pack up his writing stuff and take it to his wife Agnès's house. I didn't blame him. This was no place to live anymore. When I went to Prophet's room, I imagined he'd express his regret over that night's events and apologize to everyone, especially Seyyed, while blaming the whole thing on his personal problems and psychological crises. But when I asked him why he attacked Seyyed, he said, "Don't worry, there was no ill will there."

"If I hadn't come in, you'd have killed him!" I exclaimed.

"Not my fault," he said.

"You kicked down his door and held a knife to his throat!"

"I meant no harm."

"Do you know he has heart trouble? What if he'd had a heart attack?"

"It was a mission."

"What mission?"

"From God."

If any of the customers in Café de Phares had known Persian and accidentally overheard me telling Ra'na and Seyyed about this, they for sure would have looked at us like we'd come from outer space, and that would only be fair. Most of the customers at Café de Phares, however, were French people who had other concerns. A number of them engaged in philosophical debates about the hottest topics of the day, right here in this cafe on Sundays. During one such debate about "fear," they covered everything: from the skydiver's fear his parachute won't open, to the fear that God doesn't exist. Every type of fear came up, except for one: "What if God gives him another mission?"

Seyyed was right. That's exactly what I'd been afraid of when I asked Prophet, "What guarantee is there God won't send you after someone else tomorrow?"

As he showed me the Torah, Prophet replied, "Everything is in here."

"So maybe one day you'd come after me?"

"It's not up to me. All I can say is that an unfortunate event awaits you."

Then, gesturing to the Torah, he added, "According to the signs contained in here, the beds in Rooms 6 and 12 belong to Satan!"

Room 6 was Bénédicte's room, and Room 12 was mine!

-3-

They say the flap of a butterfly's wings in China can turn into a violent storm in Chicago. Now, what exactly the movement of the tip of Prophet's knife was turning into, I couldn't say. But one thing was clear: movement had begun!

Bénédicte, who'd given up sawing things and had been quiet for a while, set up shop in the hallway again. Every day she started at nine o'clock in the morning. She went about her work with such bitterness and rage, you'd think she was hacking the source of all her life's miseries to pieces. It was as if those famous images of hell had made their way from the underworld into this one: the Ghashiye serpent, the boiling cauldron, and the evil-doers sawn in half. Day or night, I no longer had a moment's peace.

Prophet, who rarely ventured out of his room before the incident, now went to the bathroom a hundred times a night, and my heart stopped every time he opened his door. The way he stomped his feet on the ground and moved with such urgency could only mean he was on his way to murder someone.

Around six, I'd get into bed, exhausted and on edge, but the second my eyes grew heavy, Érik François Schmidt hollered in the stairwell in his deep, booming voice: "No, Gabik, not here! Not here!"

Then came the crack of a whip, and the heart-rending howls of Gabik, who had peed on every last stair by the time he got to the building's main exit. Next up was a flock of pigeons making a racket. They'd recently come to roost on the roof of the building opposite ours and took up an ominous song, which brought back vague, anxiety-inducing memories that prevented me from sleeping.

Now that Bénédicte had reopened for business in the hallway, the scraping sound of her saw was back. I was only able to sleep for an hour, between eight and nine in the morning.

With Seyyed leaving to go to his wife Agnès's house, my relationship with Ra'na started to get depressing.

After I gave her a week to find a new place, she spent most of her time with Seyyed and only came to the kitchen to eat lunch, dinner, or sleep. Since Seyyed hadn't set foot on this floor for a few days, Ra'na spent all her time in the kitchen. Mostly she lay on the bed and stared up at the greasy, flaking ceiling. She didn't go outside or eat like before, nor did she try to find a new place for herself, though the week would be up in two days.

Once I'd eaten lunch, I'd go to Café de Phares and sit with Seyyed for a few hours. When I came home, I said goodnight to Ra'na whether I'd had dinner or not, and took up my pallette, easel, and paintbrush.

Over those few days, during the brief moments we saw each other in the hallway, nothing more than a few cold, clipped exchanges passed between us. I knew she was bored. I knew she was deeply unhappy. I knew she wanted me to take her out like I'd done before. Take her to the movies. Or at least to sit on the terrace of a cafe. But everything had been ruined between us, and nothing was the way it was before. Well, she'd made her choice.

Still, I couldn't take it. Watching people be devastated is one of the saddest sights in the world. To see someone who used to strut like a peacock now become an emaciated, featherless chicken. To see someone who thought herself a queen and you her slave, now waiting for you to give her the time of day. To see that . . .

No, I couldn't handle it. So, I took her out. We sat on the terrace of a café. We watched people pass by in silence. But there was nothing to say to each other. Later, she drank so much she was plastered and couldn't walk, so I had to prop her up to get us home. She, however, wanted to wander around, so we did. Outside a club, she put her foot down and insisted we go in to dance.

Maybe it is possible to understand people, but there are some situations that are so tragic, they're unfathomable. Now I had to endure my own grief as well as hers.

The next day when I went to the kitchen, she was lying on the bed staring at the ceiling again. I went to go heat something up to eat and noticed she hadn't eaten her food from the night before. When I asked why, she said she didn't feel like it. I told her to come eat lunch then, and she said she had no appetite. Then, as I sat down on a chair to eat my food, I saw a tear rolling down her cheek. I went to her side. As soon as I started stroking her hair, she burst into tears. She'd had a horrible panic attack. She sobbed and blamed herself for treating me so poorly. When she calmed down, we went out again. We walked around half the night and went from pub to pub drinking beer. Everywhere we went she left her glass half full. On our way back, every time we passed a pub, she wanted to go in and sit a while longer. At the end of the night, I had to drag her back home.

The next day when I went to the kitchen, she was lying in bed again. I sensed she was melting away like a candle. As I was shaving my beard, I watched her in the mirror. Beads of cold sweat stood out on her face.

"I know what's bothering you," I said.

She whipped her head in my direction, like she knew I wasn't just making small talk.

"Just say yes or no. You want my help?"

She propped herself up. Her brow was furrowed, as if she wanted to be sure she'd understood me correctly. She had, but she was still wary.

"What do you mean? How?"

"I'm headed out to meet him."

The way she threw herself back on the bed, I was sure she'd caught my full meaning. Then, she turned toward me in amazement and said, "You're a strange person!"

Yes, I was a strange person.

"Just say yes or no," I said.

She was stuck in a real predicament. On one hand, she could tell I really did want to help her, despite all the trouble she'd caused me—which was hard to believe, given the psychological dimensions of the situation—but on the other hand, her womanly sense of self-respect wouldn't allow her to show weakness by saying yes. Especially since this was the card she'd always played with me in our relationship. She'd humiliate herself now if she revealed her hand was empty. Plus, she knew her fate lay in my hands and that if she turned me down, she could kiss her dreams goodbye.

I didn't have the heart to watch her struggle anymore. Pretending to be looking in the mirror, I said, "You know how close we are. Even if he wanted to, he wouldn't do anything if he thought it might hurt our friendship. But if I convince him it's okay, things might be different. Do you want me to or not?"

Ra'na had visibly rallied. Her womanly dignity and reserved personality must have been searching for an appropriate response; and with my long speech I'd given her an opportunity. She threw her arm over her face, covering her eyes:

"You do what you think is best. Don't tell him I said anything though!"

-4-

Ingrid kept bobbing her head in a funny way, like a bird pecking at seeds. I looked everywhere but didn't see Bernard. Did that mean he didn't care?

Ingrid bobbing her head made me laugh, especially since she had to peek at the sheet music out of the corner of her eye to follow along. I never thought such a graceful, attractive girl would look so funny.

To focus on the fugue they were performing, I decided to examine the crown moldings on the wall. It didn't take long, however, before my eyes began to wander over the row of images that all looked the same, until they landed on a frame on the right side of the auditorium. My heart stopped. I was always afraid of frames on the wall, regardless of whose portrait was inside. The very fact that they would frame someone's picture meant that I could never forget all my deeds would be recorded. Here, I mostly dealt with government offices; but now, in this quiet public theater, I was reminded for the first time of the presence of a higher power. A lovely picture in a pathetic little frame. So there were monsters here too, just behind sheets of glass. Without a doubt the record of my deeds was being written. But there was no sign of the Ghashiye serpent, nor was I being sawn in half.

I was starting to hyperventilate a little bit. I had an intense urge to leave the theater, but there was no way. I was sitting in the third row and if I moved even slightly, it would disturb everyone. I tried to see how long Ingrid's score was. I couldn't tell. Looking up at the ceiling, my thoughts drifted elsewhere. Back to a small party we'd had, the very night after I exiled Ra'na to the kitchen.

•

Tipsy on wine, people were chatting in small groups in the corner. I had arrived a little late. As soon as I'd finished eating dinner, I sensed the weight of someone's gaze on my face. I spotted a beautiful girl in the corner of the room whose eyes lit up with an affectionate smile. I knew that face. And yet, it was the first time I'd seen her. Staring at her, I journeyed back in time. She must have seen me somewhere before too, since she was also staring and traveling back in time. Transported miles away from the heart of Europe, I clutched at everything that passed before my eyes, somewhere between fog and memory.

The door opened and Bernard's silhouette appeared in the frame. He, like me, was late. A few moments later when Bernard picked up his plate of food and dragged me over to him, a strange sense of unease welled up inside me. Bernard stopped in front of her: "Meet Ingrid."

As I shook her hand, our eyes met again and I was suddenly transported to a faraway city. To a hot summer's day. To high noon, when sun's rays strike the crown of the head. To a girl who had been lost in the river. To Somaylu, the tears swirling in his eyes like a whirlpool.

The light touch of a hand on my shoulder plucked me out of the burning heat of that afternoon and back to the theater. I turned. It was Seyyed, who had arrived late, and was now sitting in one of the vacant seats behind me. He flashed me a smile, the meaning of which I didn't quite understand.

When I'd seen the state Ra'na was in earlier, I called him immediately and said, "I have to see you right away."

"Come to Café de Phares," he replied. "I'll head out right now."

"I can't. Ingrid has a concert at three."

"When is it over?"

"I don't know. It's one of those concerts the city puts on for special occasions."

"Which neighborhood is it in?"

"The one right next to ours."

"Then I'll join you. We'll go to the cafe right after."

In the end, we'd set our showdown for six o'clock.

Again I tried to focus on the music. Again the bird was pecking at seeds, accompanied by an oboe and a harpsichord. The harpsichord player, a distinguished older gentleman, was sitting there perfectly still like a wax figure. Only when he had to play the high keys did he move his hands slightly. I looked up so I wouldn't see Ingrid's ridiculous bobbing. But the weight of Seyyed's presence, as he leaned forward like he was waiting for an opportunity to tell me something important, transported me to Café de Phares, where a duel like no other was set to be fought. This was to be the defining moment. Of course, he was too subtle to just let me read the expressions on his face. Over the past few years, however, I had learned that to read his thoughts, I really only had to pay attention to one part of the smiling mask he wore: the little vein over his eye.

As Ingrid's head bobbing intensified and the rhythm picked up speed, a sense that the conclusion was approaching gripped the audience, and I mentally returned to the theater.

As Seyyed was clapping, he murmured in my ear, "For the love of God, don't lose this one!" While acknowledging the outpouring of emotion from the audience, Ingrid looked around. When she spotted me she smiled, and turned back toward the harpsichord player.

"I'm going to talk to Ingrid for a minute," I told Seyyed. "Then we can go to Café de Phares."

I pushed my way against the crowd, which was headed toward the exit, and went up to the stage. The whole time my attention had been engaged elsewhere, but now I was probably going to have to give my review of their performance.

A few people had made their way up to the stage ahead of me. Ingrid was talking to a balding man. When she saw me, she came right over. She was back to being that sweet girl whose eyes radiated affection. She kissed me hello on the cheek. The man whose conversation had been interrupted was now staring at us with surprise. Ingrid's sudden move worried me.

"Well done," I said.

She blushed: "It didn't turn out the way I wanted."

"How come?"

She wiped her hand hard across her face, like she was trying to wipe off an imaginary smudge of something: "I was a little nervous."

"You could tell."

"How so?"

"You were moving around a lot."

"I was flustered."

I knew why, but a mischievous inclination forced me to dig myself deeper yet again: "Why?"

She laughed and put her hand on my shoulder: "Well, with you here . . ."

With you here! Ha! With me here, or with Pavarotti here? Poor Ingrid! To change the subject I said, "So Bernard didn't show?"

"He went to see the studio."

"What studio?"

"Didn't he tell you?"

"Tell me what?"

"He made a deal with a record company. We have to start rehearsals in a day or two."

I brought my cigarette up to my lips. When I went to light it, her sweet eyes stared directly into mine: "If you can't quit, at least cut back. This is the greatest opportunity of our lives!"

I lit the cigarette and unconsciously turned my head. Once again, the picture frame caught my eye.

-5-

A deathly silence had descended upon the sixth floor of Érik François Schmidt's building. Even the bell of the Saint-Paul Saint-Louis Church, which should have struck ten o'clock at this very moment, was quiet. After gathering up the sawdust and putting her little carpentry supplies in a corner, Bénédicte withdrew to her room at eight o'clock, as usual. There was no sign of Prophet, however, who was now the undisputed nighttime ruler of the floor. It was as if Ra'na had packed up all the madness of our building into her suitcase and taken it with her when she left. Something ended with her departure. Yet everything testified to the fact that this silence was pregnant with something else, like the silence after a coup. Only on the following day was it becoming clear how much everyone had lost in the ghastly silence of the night before.

Not a peep was coming from Prophet's room. Not a glass marble hitting the floor, his brushstrokes against the wall, or even the unpleasant sound of him clearing his throat. I'd gotten used to Kalantar and Ali not being around much, since they mostly worked in hotels as nighttime security guards. Emmanuelle, too, returned to the third floor at night, to her family. If only Fereydoon would turn up, who'd vanished into thin air. Or if only Milosh and his punk friends would come home, get high, and laugh their heads off again so the whole building could hear.

Now, if Prophet was lurking behind the stairwell wall or in the narrow hallway, waiting for me when I went to the kitchen or the bathroom, who would take my dead body away?

I suddenly felt like I'd fallen into a trap. A mysterious hand had first skillfully cleared out my surroundings so there was no one within earshot, then prepared an ambush so, when the time came, it could stab me in the back.

It was no coincidence that Prophet kept quiet. No hunter announces his presence when it's time to pounce. Over and over, he succumbs to the little death that happens in the set time between breathing in and out. He does this so effectively, his prey senses the void of his absence in every atom of the surrounding air. Right when the prey relaxes and goes pleasantly numb, that's the moment to strike. Unfortunately, as a hunter myself who knew the unbreakable rules of the hunt all too well, it could only make me anxious that the hunter was silent and nowhere to be found. I was going to die, and I didn't even get to go pleasantly numb first. What an awful day! And what an even more awful night!

At noon when I woke up, first it was the incident with Ra'na, who was in dire straits, then Ingrid's concert, with her ominous news, and finally, the meeting with Seyyed, where I was just starting to realize I'd dug my own grave.

When the waiter brought our cups of coffee over, he set them down on the table like he was the arbiter bringing us the weapons of war. Now that he'd stepped back to observe us, it seemed the battle was supposed to begin.

Unlike the other tables in Café de Phares, a heavy silence lingered over our table. Seyyed had set up shop there, like an opponent assured of victory from the very start. That smiling mask and magnetic aura of his had once again returned to his face. He didn't seem concerned at all, though I'd told him I had something important to discuss.

The waiter was still standing there, staring. His two thin lips curled into a mischievous smile. I slapped my hands on the table and stared directly into Seyyed's face: "This girl is losing it!"

Seyyed pulled back as he scowled. Did that mean he was truly surprised? Or had he only just realized the initial look on his face was a tactical error?

"She hasn't eaten for three days," I said. "She just lies there on the bed and stares up at the ceiling."

The twitch of the little vein over his eye told me he now knew where I was going with this.

"I know you like her too," I said.

The muscles of Seyyed's face contorted into an entirely different expression: "If I bring her to my room, it's so she won't bother you!"

In attic rooms, nobody has any privacy. Personal affairs, like the bathroom on this floor, very quickly turn into public matters. Ra'na would still bother me at all hours with any excuse, even after I, operating like the Israelis on the Land for Peace policy, relinquished the kitchen to her to regain my independence; and Seyyed was in the loop on all the details of the case. The third night after I gave up the kitchen to Ra'na in the interests of peace, and exactly thirteen days before Prophet's attack on Seyyed, I had just gotten back into the flow of my work when Ra'na got bored again and came to my room. A bit later, when Seyyed came back from seeing his wife or someone else, he stopped by to ask how I was doing, as usual, before heading to his room. Seeing my irritable mood, he got up to leave.

"Sit down, I'll bring some tea," I said.

"I have to go. I want to type up what I just wrote."

Sensing her chance, Ra'na said, "If you want, I can help you. My typing's not bad."

Seyyed hesitated, and the thin vein over his left eye twitched.

"It's just a few pages. I type pretty well myself."

Her efforts coming to naught, Ra'na was deflated. But Seyyed, who had been on his way out, stayed for another half hour for no reason, just to be nice. Then when he was about to leave, he turned to Ra'na and said, "Did you really mean it? About your offer."

Ra'na's eyes nearly popped out of their sockets.

"Absolutely. That way I'll have something to keep me busy."

From that night on, Ra'na was in Seyyed's room most nights, and although our evening chess matches had fallen apart, in exchange, I got a bit of my peace and quiet back. Seyyed wasn't too displeased himself. He'd made a big sacrifice, but in return he became extraordinarily productive. If before he wrote a few lines once in a while, now he finished a new story every night and Ra'na typed it up gleefully all night long.

The waiter at Café de Phares was looking at me. I put my hands back on the table and looked Seyyed directly in the face: "That's not the issue. We have to save her from this situation."

"And I won't get into trouble if I do?"

"As far as I'm concerned, your conscience should be clear."

"I wouldn't do anything that I know would hurt a friend."

"You can rest assured I don't have any particular attachment to her. Any special attentions I pay her are out of pity."

The thin vein over Seyyed's left eye twitched. Laying extra emphasis on the words "particular attachment,' he laughed: "And how do we know that she has a particular attachment to me?"

"Let's go," I said. Leaving two ten-franc coins on the table, I added, "Her problem is you! She told me not to say anything, though."

The waiter came up and smiled at me as he picked up the coins.

As we left the cafe, a cold wind blew dry leaves in our faces.

A black cloud had enveloped the autumnal Parisian sky. The rain could start falling any moment. Coming up to our building door, Seyyed suddenly stopped short: "That psycho won't come and put a knife to our throats again, will he?"

"So you've realized I'm leading you to the slaughter!"

"I'd come with you even if you were taking me to hell."

-6-

Ever since the night of the incident, the building was dead silent, and *Carmen* no longer emanated from Emmanuelle's room. If not for the occasional sound of Milosh's cello, I'd have thought the movement of Prophet's knife tip had killed something on this floor. Something whose head was in Seyyed's room and whose legs were in Milosh and Emmanuelle's rooms.

I couldn't be bothered to do anything. I just lay there on the bed, staring at the ceiling. My stomach was empty but I had no desire to go to the kitchen. It was a graveyard now.

When I came home with him around sunset, Seyyed turned right on the sixth floor and knocked on the kitchen door. I turned left and went to my room. I stretched out on the bed and picked up *Burnt Treasure*, which I'd just recently got a hold of, and opened it to a random page. It was a field report from Maxime Pic, the first representative from the Gramophone company to come to Iran during the reign of Mozaffar al-Din Shah:

> *Iranians are a race born for commerce. They are clever and quick-witted, but their way of thinking and making transactions is entirely Asian. They make excuses in all things and delay everything. A promise made by an Iranian lacks a strong backing, and telling untruths is a forgivable offense. The women are extremely profligate, and they buy anything that attracts their interest without reference to the price. In some respects, Iranians are like children. They desire to be amazed and astounded. New, noisy, or shiny things grab their attention . . .*

Bénédicte's cat crying right outside my door broke my concentration. I edged the door open slightly. Silence in the hall. The cat stared at me reproachfully. I turned partway around. Then I went and knocked on the kitchen door. When Seyyed opened it, I was embarrassed and apologized as I came in, like a pimp on his first day on the job. I pulled two cans of beer out of the fridge and offered them to them. Then I filled the kettle, put it on the stove, and like a pimp who'd been on the job for years, I made my way toward the door and said, "When it boils, steep it yourself."

I got back into bed. I wasn't up for Maxime Pic. I picked up *The Book of Disquiet* by Fernando Pessoa: "I have created various personalities within myself. I create these personalities continuously. All my dreams, the moment they pass through my mind, take on the form of existence, without any losses or imperfections, through someone else who dreams the same dream as me. It occurs through them, not me. In order to create myself, I have destroyed the self."

I haven't read any further than that for a while. Every time I get to the lines I underlined, I close the book and stare at the cover. Fernando Pessoa is a shadow crossing the street on the blurry cobblestones, which look sort of like cracked dirt in a desert. In his frightened eyes, there is a message, and every time I am drawn to my desk drawer to uncover it.

I open the drawer and for the thousandth time, take out the leather-bound notebook of memoirs the ex-officer left me in his will. My eye lights upon the dedication on the first page, and with a sentimental smile, I page through the notebook:

"Khatoun was pretty much the luckiest woman in the entire world. She lost her mother as soon as she was born. The placenta was stuck inside the womb, and the midwife handed the child to her mother so she could tie the umbilical cord.

"Khatoun's mother let out a scream and in the next moment, her gaze darted like a terrified swallow toward the dim light of morning fluttering outside the window.

"Three years later, her father also died, and little Khatoun had no choice but to go to her aunt's house. Auntie's house wasn't bad, but it wasn't long before Auntie herself died, and nine-year-old Khatoun moved to her elder uncle's house. Uncle, a forty-year-old man, smoked his pipe all night long and stared into the darkness in the corner of the yard. Eventually the vague rumors that had taken hold amongst his acquaintances reached Uncle. Gripped by fear, he searched high and low to find a husband for Khatoun, but failed. Now the whispers were making the rounds among the villagers.

"The older Khatoun got, the more sickly and pale the village boys became. At night, vague, feverish whispers occupied the space between mouths and ears: 'Don't look at that beautiful face of hers, my son. I've seen for myself she's got six fingers!'

"'So what if she does? Look at her eyes and her rosy cheeks. Look how tall she is!'

"'Her every step is the step of Death! Think of her poor mother, who she killed during her birth. Then the untimely death of her father, and even her ill-fated aunt!'

"Six years later, Uncle passed away too, and fifteen-year-old Khatoun had to move once more.

"The day her younger uncle brought her to his house, his hand trembled so badly when he went to open the door, the latch made a clicking noise.

"Khatoun burst into tears and ran toward the river. On the edge of the water, her uncle took her in his arms and pressed his wet cheek to her flowery headscarf, his shoulders shaking.

"The next day, her uncle sold everything he owned, took her by the hand, and spirited her away somewhere the prying eyes of acquaintances wouldn't be able to reach."

The rest of the memoirs were about their relationship with the ex-officer. Whenever the ex-officer—who was thirty-five when he ended up in jail, and fifty when he got out—came home from work, he would cook and invite his friends over. He'd taken risks all those years and gone to prison for so long in order to heal his old wounds. Now that one of them had opened up again, he had healed it in a risk-free "war" that featured pots, stools, and plates.

"Khatoun and her uncle were right there in the trenches helping too," the ex-officer wrote. "Whenever a suitor appeared though, the issue of the sixth finger would always come up just as we were about to close the deal.

"Finally, one night when Khatoun's uncle lay on his death bed, I, who had failed in my every effort to ensure Khatoun's future prosperity, renounced my good name and reputation, called her in and sat her down at the foot of her uncle's bed: 'I've been like a father to you, but if you wish, I can also be your husband.'

"Holding her trembling hands up to my face, she sobbed violently and said, 'I have no one in this world but you and Uncle!'"

That very night, twenty-three-year-old Khatoun was wed to the fifty-year-old ex-officer. When the ceremony was over, Khatoun's uncle rested his head on the officer's shoulder and wept.

"I never figured out," the ex-officer commented in his memoirs, "whether Uncle's tears that night were tears of joy, or something else."

Somebody was knocking on my door. Nervously I hid the notebook under the mattress and opened the door.

"Please come to the kitchen for a minute," Seyyed said in a hushed tone.

Seyyed spoke in the same tone in the kitchen. The tip of Prophet's knife had left no safe quarter.

"We're leaving."

Ra'na's suitcase was in the middle of the kitchen, and Ra'na stood beside it with an expectant air. My gaze was fixed on the handle, and so was Seyyed's.

He looked away from the suitcase: "I thought I'd take Ra'na to Agnès's house. She shouldn't stay here with that nut job."

Then he grabbed the suitcase and set out. Regret and gratitude mingled on Ra'na's face, a look she had cleverly chosen to avoid seeming insincere. This look was supposed to replace words, which would have sounded disingenuous, but her mask seemed equally forced.

On the first-floor landing, they looked up to say goodbye for the final time. Our heads and arms quickly went through a ridiculous series of movements that only arise in moments when words have lost all meaning.

And now, two hours after Seyyed and Ra'na left, nothing could pierce the deathly stillness that had enveloped Érik François Schmidt's building. Even the roots of Bénédicte's potted plants refused to move. If this silence lasted any longer, I was sure to lose my mind, but the sound of a finger tapping on my door made me freeze in place.

-7-

The remnants of the light are slowly fading. He's still sitting in the chair. Motionless. All I see now is the vague outline of his face. The thicker the air grows, the more this vague outline resembles M.A.R.'s face. That means . . .

She could have told me! Did I not let her? Why did she make no effort?

Why would she make an effort? So I could be tormented even more than before? When had she ever tormented anyone?

But she had! She tormented me. She was simply a mirror that reflected my image back to me. And this distorted, inaccurate image made me hate myself.

We'd gone to a party. One of the ambassadors' houses. Everyone there was either an ambassador or a big shot. In those days, I was still somebody. I hadn't yet chosen smoking and drinking over singing. M.A.R. had made something of herself too. She was an actress and a model.

We'd known each other for barely a week. She wore a stunning dress that night, and I was delighted that her beauty and grace would enhance my credibility. When my song was over, I got up to grab a drink. The Indian Minister of Culture appeared in front of me, and before I knew what was happening, he subjected me to an extended monologue on the status of Persian language in India and the impact of Iranian poets and artists immigrating there.

For one second I lost focus, and M.A.R. had taken off her shoes and sat down on the edge of the fountain in the middle of the courtyard.

She was just doing her own thing, while I, worried about what other people would think, was frantically looking around for her shoes.

I threw her shoes down in front of her and hissed at her, out of earshot of everyone else, that if she wasn't more mindful of her behavior, I'd refuse to see her again.

A little later when they summoned everyone to dinner, M.A.R. was nowhere to be found. Foolishly I imagined she'd been upset and left quietly so as not to damage my reputation any further.

Nervous as I left the ambassador's elegant mansion, I noticed a large pool in the middle of the expansive grounds, which had been empty when we arrived but now had something fluttering in it. I froze. With the blue pool walls behind her, her silky dress was bobbing in the waves, mesmerizing me. I saw a tiny water sprite from a faraway land who'd been exiled to this empty pool. Yearning for that long-lost sea, she sang a mournful tune.

Once I was sure I wasn't dreaming, her enchanting movements forced me to admire her against my will. And when I came back to myself, realizing we were in the Italian ambassador's home, I remembered my own reputation and was overtaken by anger: "What did you get in the pool for?"

Walking in the middle of it, she murmured with childlike innocence, "I saw it was empty, thought I'd fill it."

I envied her. While I was worried about everyone else's opinion, she'd liberated herself from the constraints of judgment. I lived with the image of myself that I wanted others to see, while she lived without an image.

Her presence made it obvious how two-faced I was. I'd grabbed her arm and dragged her out of the house without a word.

•

Now all that's left is me, and the thick, murky remnants of the day. He's still sitting in the chair. The darker the room gets, the more the vague, blurry outline of his face resembles M.A.R.

We're sitting. As if both of us are waiting for the fateful moment. Like those nights during the bombings, when we sat in the dark, waiting for death, unclear when it would arrive and from what quarter.

-8-

Since the night of Prophet's attack, every knock on the door was like a warning bell that plunged me into anxiety. I told Ra'na we should knock very lightly whenever we needed something to avoid causing a commotion. Ra'na replied with terror: "No, it'll remind me of the way Prophet knocked that night."

"Okay, very softly then, three times. Every time, three knocks."

And now that someone was knocking, I suddenly understood what torture Ra'na had endured all through the night until morning. It may have been the first time I ever understood her.

Once again I heard someone softly tapping on my door. If only I had a peephole, I thought, then I could easily look outside and stop my imagination from running wild. I went to the door: "Who is it?"

I was so afraid, my voice caught in my throat. The sound of a familiar cough came from the hallway: "It's me, Ali."

Slowly, I opened the door. Ali pulled back a little with his usual shyness, "Am I disturbing you?"

Not only was he not disturbing me, he'd rescued this building, which had been sucked down into a whirlpool of terror and silence, from the depths. The roots of Bénédicte's potted plants would resume growing. I picked up the key to the kitchen and said quietly, "Let's go over here."

Ever since Ali had joined the brotherhood of mystics, he'd completely changed. He walked slowly. He talked mildly, and when he went to turn a key in a lock, he did it so deliberately, it seemed as if the door opened with a whisper. Precisely the opposite of Prophet, who pounded the walls with invisible waves of tension and anxiety every step he took.

I closed the kitchen door and offered him a seat. He sat on the very edge of the chair, as if to assure me that he had absolutely no wish to disturb me and would leave shortly. Then he shifted in his seat a bit and said with a smile full of warmth and embarrassment, "Have you heard from Seyyed? I keep calling but he never picks up."

"After that whole thing went down, he went to his wife Agnès's house."

"What thing?"

"The thing with Prophet."

"The thing with Prophet?"

"Haven't you heard?"

"No, I was out of town."

Ali had a special relationship with Seyyed. Unlike Seyyed, who came here before the revolution, Ali had to escape Iran over the mountains. Once here, he faced quite a few hurdles to get back on his feet. The usual issues—the days of exile stretching out interminably and the signs of one's failure becoming inescapable—coincided with his personal failure in love with a French girl. Seyyed was warm, kind and stable, and his presence during this series of disasters was a godsend. To make the most of Seyyed's comforting presence, Ali usually cooked, and when noon rolled around, he knocked on Seyyed's door to invite him to lunch. After that they went to the movies or a cafe.

When Seyyed and I met, we started spending a lot of time together, which changed the course of Ali's life. Now it was Seyyed who woke me up around midday with a phone call: "Your coffee's ready." When he came in, he set the coffee down in front of me and made lunch while we smoked cigarettes and chatted. Then we played a few games of chess and went to Café de Phares in the evening. At dusk everyone went about their business, and late at night there was more chess, which we played frenetically until dawn.

Things being the way they were, there really was no chance for Seyyed to spend time with Ali. Now this pain was added to all of Ali's previous disappointments—he had come to rely heavily on Seyyed's presence. He grew bitter, never slept at night and was constantly arguing with hotel guests. When the hotel owner heard about the guests' complaints, Ali was fired. Worst of all, when he found out about our nightly chess games, he seemed to be on the verge of tears.

Every time Seyyed passed by Ali's door—which he had to do whenever he needed to go to the bathroom—Ali would clear his throat loudly to remind Seyyed of his presence. And if Seyyed ignored these strange and pitiful cries for attention, then a barrage of notes would come flying under the door to his room: "I've been trying to sleep for two hours but your racket is keeping me awake!" or "Who flushes their toilet at midnight! I've taken sleeping pills a few times and every time you wake me up!"

One night I asked Seyyed, "Isn't this the same kind of love Rumi had for his beloved Shams?"

"Recently," said Seyyed, "Ali ran into one of the guys from his old unit on the street who wound up joining the brotherhood of mystics. His former war buddy, now a mystic, told him, 'Come on, let me take you somewhere, so you can understand what love is.'"

Ali went, and when he'd understood what love was, a better job was made available for him in a better hotel. Now he spent most of his time typing up pamphlets in the same style as the political pamphlets he wrote for his old organization and publishing them for the brotherhood. He slept well at night. His disappointed hopes didn't bother him anymore, nor did the departure of that girl, which had destroyed his life, nor the unpleasant news coming out of Iran, nor the absence of Seyyed, who now had other things to keep him occupied. From then on, he saw Seyyed once in a while, and even then, it was only to try to entice Seyyed into these new worlds. That's it.

Now, when he heard about the incident between Seyyed and Prophet, not one iota of his peace of mind was disturbed. He curled his hand under his chin, leaned back on the chair, and said, as though it had been nothing more than a few flies squabbling with each other, "It's just about orbits! When an atom falls out of orbit, it may temporarily cause a disturbance, but the disturbance is for the atom, not for the orbit. This very disturbance is in fact a requirement for the existence of the nucleus. The world is based upon orbits. From the tiniest atom to the entirety of existence . . ."

As he repeated, parrot-like, the teachings of his spiritual guide, I said to myself, "If only I too could surrender myself to the teachings of a man who held a doctorate in nuclear physics, but instead of building some kind of power plant or bomb in his home country for the people who faced a thousand issues due to a shortage of all things nuclear, he preferred to set up shop over here and sell tranquility to people who had everything except a 'world in orbit.'"

As my ill luck would have it though, in those days when I could still surrender myself to someone, I met a man who would shatter all my hopes and dreams.

He wore a cloak and turban, but nothing about him suited that outfit. He was fifty-five and still lived in that small hovel from his student days. No one in the seminary knew him by the title Hojjat al-Islam. In a place where everyone was preoccupied with the rituals of ablution, he had immersed himself in the Illuminationist philosophy of Sohravardi, the metaphysics of Molla Sadra, and tragedies of Sophocles. Whenever he came to my house, he sat and talked with my wife, who wasn't wearing a veil, just as he would with a man.

He didn't drink anything himself, but keeping careful watch, he would fill our teacups deliberately and gracefully when they were empty. When his travels took him to western Iran, one of the cults there came to see him: "We were promised you would come."

"It's a lie."

"We were told you'd deny it," they said, falling at his feet.

So, he'd stayed, out of necessity. This was the only dark age in his life that I didn't understand. Finally, I threw caution to the wind one day: "It doesn't seem like you'd be one of those snake oil peddlers!"

He filled my empty glass.

"I'm no doctor, engineer, or writer. If they imagine I have some remedy for their incurable pain, why should I withhold it from them?"

"Is it true they eat fire and don't burn? They hook themselves up to electricity and nothing happens?"

"It's true."

"Do you do these things too?"

"I can't."

"How come?"

"They're able to do it because of their belief in me. Who should I believe in?"

From the very moment he came into my room, Ali had perched himself so close to the edge of the chair, I was sure he would leave at the first sign of the slightest inconvenience. He must have noticed me staring into space and so stood up. It suddenly crossed my mind that the key to the Mehdi conundrum might lie with him. After all, he was one of the long-time inhabitants of this floor.

"Do you know anyone here called Mehdi?"

"Everyone here has a few different names. My name's Ali, but they used to call me Haydar. Majid for a while too."

Then, with a shy smile, he added, "Before we all went our separate ways, of course. Kalantar's name is Majid, but he was called Hossein as well. Mohsen was another name of his. They called Taqi, who used to live in your room, both Ali and Mohammad. I don't know about Prophet. I just know that his name is Hassan. I also heard Fereydoon called Morteza once or twice. For a while, Seyyed's nickname was Cyrus, but Mehdi . . . No. I don't know anyone by that name."

My head was spinning. The sixth floor of Érik François Schmidt's building, the number of tenants of which had suddenly multiplied, was drowning in a crowd of persons unknown, all of whom looked alike.

-9-

My eyes were just about to close when a strange sound dragged me out of bed. When I opened the door, a cloud of white dust wafted into my room. I quickly closed the door and, as I coughed, pondered the ghost who was now standing in the open door of Fereydoon's room, wearing a white sheet and wielding an electric sander like it was a machine gun.

Ever since the night of the incident, my life had been turned upside down. Every sound from Prophet's room was a warning sign that sent me into a panic. As soon as I heard the glass marble hitting the floor, I waited for his next move so I could predict what had been revealed to him this time. With every tap of Jean Jaurès's bed, which had now become the place where revelations came down from up on high, I would wait for him to open his door. If he opened it, I held my breath, and I didn't relax until I heard the sharp, piercing sound of his footsteps move away. My bed was Satan's bed, and unfortunate events awaited me. Accordingly, I marshalled all my senses so as to infer from a few random sounds the exact moment the order for my assassination had been issued.

I was like a condemned prisoner whose death was certain, but the date and time were not. Every key that turned in a lock, every footstep that approached, every knock on a door; any of these could signify the end of everything. A horrible death which, sometimes a faint ember of hope made tolerable: "The room has been rented to him temporarily, and the lease Érik François Schmidt gave him could be coming to an end any day." Until that day, however, I had to be on constant alert. I had to find out what relationship the tags around his neck, which looked like dog tags, had to his divine mission. I had to figure out what his attack on Seyyed and Ra'na had to do with me, and what all that had to do with the mysteriously incognito Mehdi.

And now that Fereydoon, his close friend, had returned, I had to be on the lookout for an opportunity to pull him aside into the kitchen, away from the prying eyes of Prophet. Maybe by solving parts of this mystery, I could restore my long-lost nights of calm.

I desperately needed to sleep. Over the past few days, I'd been hit hard by terrible insomnia. I slid under the covers, but it felt like Fereydoon was using his electric sander on my face. And every time he turned it off for a second, Bénédicte's grinding saw from down below carried the torturous rhythm forward like the percussion section of an ear-splitting orchestra. My luck couldn't get worse than this. These were my days and nights.

At six in the morning, by which time sleep had slowly begun to overpower me, Érik François Schmidt's angry shout woke me up: "No Gabik! Not here!" Next came the pigeons: "Coo coo, coo coo coo coo." They repeated this ominous melody so much, I was reminded of the day a mob gathered in our street, their fists clenched as they screamed to the same rhythm: "Off, off! Off with his head!" They dragged the man who lived across from us out of his basement and . . .

When the grind of Bénédicte's saw crescendoed, I was sure those men with their clenched fists had flown across the ocean to punish me, the man whose bed belonged to Satan.

I envied Seyyed as I squeezed the pillow to my head. Now that I thought about it, I didn't blame Ra'na for preferring him. True, Prophet had threatened Seyyed with his knife. Seyyed didn't have problems like I did, though, and in fact, he was much better off than before. He no longer had to court Ra'na in secret, and he lived like a king. At night, his wife Agnès took care of him, and in the morning, when Agnès went to the office, Ra'na did. Instead of listening to the grating sound of Bénédicte's saw and the pigeons' calls of "Off with his head," he heard Miles Davis's trumpet first thing every morning. Then, a delicate hand would run itself through his hair. When he opened his eyes, long locks of sweet-smelling hair glided over his cheek. Then, teeth gently grazed his earlobe, "Your coffee is ready."

Scrape, scrape. Scrape, scrape.

"Ugh, Bénédicte, at least nail the things you're cutting together so I'll get to hear the sound of a hammer once in a while too!"

Scrape, scrape. Scrape, scrape.

When the electric sander started up again, I hopped out of bed in a flash. I opened the door and made my way down the hall to the kitchen through a torrent of white dust, weaving acrobatically in and out of Bénédicte's various boards and pieces of wood. I picked up the receiver and dialed Ingrid's number. Fortunately, she wasn't home, and I was able to say my piece to her answering machine without getting in trouble: "I know the lengths Bernard has gone to for this opportunity, but I've decided to go back to Iran. I hope you'll forgive me!"

-10-

For the first time, I saw that Murnau's Faust and his partner had both disappeared. I was panicking. Don't tell me they've already issued their verdict! Terrified, I yelled, "What should I have done? That damn shadow had taken my place. If it were you, wouldn't you have constantly tried to beat it down too?"

"You call this beating it down?"

"I wanted to be rid of it."

"You did get rid of it, in the end!"

"I didn't believe it. I didn't know which of us was which anymore."

"But you saw your reflection."

"I hadn't seen it for so long, I didn't recognize myself. Besides, if that were my intention . . ."

A finger poked me in the forehead: "If you weren't up to something, you never would have gone to those attic rooms!"

When the ex-officer died, Khatoun went to live with her eldest daughter. The ex-officer, who didn't believe in superstitions, had decided to give Khatoun so many children that the feeling of loneliness would be put out of her mind forever. The first child was a girl, the second a boy, the third another girl, the fourth child was stillborn, and the fifth caught the measles at one year old and died. When the sixth child, who was no more than three, was run over by a car, the ex-officer suddenly recalled his uncle's tears on his death bed and started to have doubts.

"There was a fig tree in the middle of the yard," the ex-officer wrote in his memoir. "At night I smoked in the dark and stared at a black spot between the branches of the fig tree. When Khatoun saw the change that had come over me, she would bury her face in her pillow so I wouldn't hear her crying."

When the youngest daughter got married, a son-in-law was added to Khatoun's family. Then, two years later, her son started a business and got married too. With the birth of a granddaughter, Khatoun's family tree, which had been withering, started to blossom again. Now, in addition to going to her eldest daughter's house, she could go to her daughter-in-law's house or her son-in-law's house sometimes, play with her little grandchild and forget about the feeling of loneliness forever. A few years later, when the ex-officer died peacefully, the baseless rumor that had dogged Khatoun from childhood died with him. But in those days, the political situation was getting chaotic, and one day, the eldest daughter joined a flood of people who were chanting in the street and throwing their clenched fists up into the air.

A few months later, the eldest daughter gave her life to topple the monarchical regime, and Khatoun, who had spent her entire life moving from house to house like a nomad, packed up her things once more and went to her son's house.

Three years later, her son also gave his life, this time to overthrow the regime that his older sister had put in place. Now Khatoun was in Paris. In my house! And I, being superstitious to the core, suddenly saw that the place I was standing in was near the end of a closed loop, and only then did I realize the bitter irony underlying the ex-officer's dedication in his memoirs. On the first page, he had scribbled, "Dedicated to dear Mr. Yadollah, long may he live!"

Startled, I asked Faust, "But, you believe in fate and all that kind of stuff, right?"

"No questions!" Faust said resolutely.

What could I say? All night long, my wife buried her face in the pillow, crying her eyes out, and in the morning, as soon as she'd forced down a tiny bit of food, lay back down on the couch and spent the whole day staring at the pathetic candleholders near the window. One thought kept bouncing around inside her skull like a trapped bug: "She brings death wherever she goes! From the moment she set foot inside our house, we've been looking for coffins!" Then, as if to shoo the offending insect, she waved her hand in the air. A moment later, the trapped bug bounced off the wall of her skull again.

Khatoun would sit in a corner of the room all day, stroking the fibers of the carpet. She picked out a strand of hair or a thin woolen thread, and then rubbed it between her thumb and forefinger with superhuman focus, as if she wanted to untangle all the knots and straighten out all the kinks in her life. Finally, when the thread curled up and was more tangled than ever, she threw it away. She looked at her daughter's teary eyes, sighed, smoothed her white hair back off her forehead and cheeks, and tucked it under her black headscarf. Then she picked out another thread.

It was hard to open the door when I came home. The thick air of sorrow, which kept growing denser, crushed me under its weight the moment I walked in. Seconds after coming inside, I'd flop down like a corpse on a bed in the other room. In this house, it seemed, life could only go on from a horizontal position.

"As you already know," I explained to Faust and his partner, "it was a small apartment. It was just two rooms. My wife and daughter slept in one room, Khatoun in the other. Seeing the shadow of Death over my shoulder, I would smoke all night in my room in the dark, and if I could, I walked around sometimes. I saw that they couldn't sleep. One night, distraught, I held my head in my hands. Khatoun burst into tears: 'It's too crowded with me here. All night long I beg God for death.'

"From then on," I continued, "I would go out at night, walking around until dawn. Or, if Seyyed was around, I played chess. One night, my wife screamed, her whole body shaking, 'All I have in this whole world is my mother, and you can't even stand the sight of her?'

"What could I say? In this world nobody has anything but their mother, and I didn't even have that. Really, what could I say. At the very most, I could have spent all night staring at a black spot between the fig tree branches, like the ex-officer did in his final years. I had no yard here, though, and no fig tree. So I stared at a black spot on the chessboard instead. My nightly absences continued, and one night, my wife broke every bowl and plate in the house. Then when she calmed down, she wiped away her tears, saying, 'Let's go get a divorce, I can't stand a cheater!' Unable to find a better explanation for my nightly absences than cheating, I realized divorce was probably the best solution to free myself from this cycle of death. I said, 'Let's go.' And we went. By retreating to those attic rooms, I had miraculously extracted myself from the loop. And you ask why I went there?"

"When those attic rooms were on the verge of becoming a slaughterhouse," said Faust, "you could have gone back to stay with your wife."

"My wife had since passed away," I told them.

"But there was Khatoun! Instead you cleared that place out and put her in the old folks' home."

"I wanted the state to take care of her expenses, so the last thread connecting us would be broken."

"Poor Khatoun! In that case, it turns out you were the harbinger of death for them."

"Well yes . . ." I replied, "My wife said as much. She thought I was sleeping, but I heard it with my own ears."

"If you really thought that, why did you go see Khatoun once a week?"

Khatoun was the kindest woman in the world. All week she set aside the fruit they gave her for dessert so when I came to see her, she would have something to offer me. Her fear was also the most understandable thing in the world: the fear of being alone. Ever since she'd come to Paris, she made every effort to convey to me in her silent language that her existence wasn't totally useless. So whenever I came to her house, she received me like a fourteen-year-old girl would her beloved. When I got up to go, she saw my confused face as I scanned the tiny, cramped apartment. She'd look at me, completely self-assured, and say: "Looking for your keys?" Then, pointing at the space between the cushions, under the couch, or some other hiding place, she would smile triumphantly: "They're right here!"

"Well, that poor old woman, all alone . . ." I said.

A bundle of pages landed without a sound in the circle of light, and Murnau's Faust reappeared right afterwards. It seemed like the slanted light was the key to their appearance, and they were only visible when they stood under it.

Faust picked up the bundle of pages: "If we keep going on like this, in the end you'll start thinking you'll get a hold of something, no matter what it takes—a Kashani carpet, a few tins of caviar, or at least, a few kilos of 'Alaa pistachios—and in your mind, be done with this business. It seems you don't believe in anything!"

He was right. It had crossed my mind dozens of times to bribe them with something to save my own skin. I was waiting for some kind of signal from them to go ahead. I scratched the tip of my nose: "Actually, I still can't believe it. It's not unusual for exiles to be paranoid."

Faust glanced at his partner. I was afraid the Native American, who was standing outside the visibility zone again, would grab something heavy and smash it over my head so I might start believing. Holding my arms up to protect my face, I asked, "What do I need to tell you about?"

Faust waved the packet of papers in the air: "You must recognize these pages. One of your friends would bring you the paper from his office. The Toshiba logo is on the top of every page."

"Yeah, it really bugged me when I was writing it. Paper should be totally blank."

"Is this version true, or the one you wrote in your book?"

I had written *Woodwind Harmony* years ago, way before all that stuff happened. A totally made-up story. I didn't know any of the characters, in those days. Not even Seyyed or Ra'na. Then my life started to mirror the book. After Prophet's attack, I stopped going to work. As a result, I didn't have paint lying around anymore. I said I was painting, but really, I was editing the book most nights. There were two reasons for this: first, I wanted to change the fate that awaited me by rewriting the plot (an effort that was sadly unsuccessful, since I very quickly realized I had to either ruin my book or ruin my life). Second, after Seyyed and Ra'na somehow caught wind I was writing the book, every time we saw each other they tried to figure out what I'd written, and at the same time, they tried to justify or twist the events of the past, so I would revise my judgment. Well, you know a writer should have some sympathy for his protagonists, so I watered things down or adjusted them a bit, especially because the way they acted put me in a most enjoyable position: I saw that their fear of literature was stronger than the fear of Judgment Day.

"The pages with the Toshiba logo tell the unvarnished truth," I said.

Two large, powerful hands lifted me up by the shoulders and pulled the knife out of my back: "But not the whole story!"

Faust turned his head as if he were waiting to hear the answer to a question the Native American had asked. Although I hadn't been able to feel any pain, I felt relaxed now that they'd pulled the knife out. Thanking them, I said, "Look, I made a mistake in my life, which now I regret like a dog."

"Don't try to dodge the question."

"Well it's just that, isn't it a bit unfair nobody ever published my book while I was alive, and I'm still paying for the little mistakes in it now?"

Faust threw the bundle of papers on the ground, "You asked for it! We were going to send you back without a word!"

-11-

Seyyed took a swig of his coffee: "What's the situation like?"

Things on our floor were kind of like a country post-revolution. Kalantar's faction had risen to power, Seyyed was on the run, and I was stuck sitting at home like a deposed general.

Once Fereydoon was finished painting his room and building the wooden loft, he offered to help Bénédicte, who had now added construction work to her resume, and she took him up on his offer, which was like a dream come true for her. Fereydoon was thirty and Bénédicte was forty-seven. When I saw Fereydoon working in Bénédicte's room, I let out a heavy sigh in anticipation of fresh catastrophes ahead, knowing full well the fate of relationships between members of opposite sex who were also neighbors.

All day long the orchestra of electric saws, hand saws, electric sanders, hammers and nails was at work building a better life. Occasionally, this symphony of percussion instruments and power tools was accompanied by the sound of Emmanuelle enjoying *Carmen,* the unnerving moans of Kalantar's wife, or Ali's mournful chanting.

I said, "Things have calmed down again, but . . ."

"But what?"

I was dying to play a game of chess, but all my efforts to make it seem like things were fine went out the window when I said, "There've been some strange phone calls lately."

"Strange how?"

"Somebody called from America asking for Mehdi."

Shocked, Seyyed sat back in his chair: "Wow, things are out of control!"

"I didn't know you went by a fake name too!"

He was deeply taken aback, like he'd been accused of a heinous crime: "I don't understand what you mean."

"Don't worry. I'm just moving my knight a bit. Like you, who sometimes move your knight three by three or two by four, instead of three by two."

"Okay, one time I make a mistake moving my knight and now . . ."

"Then let me zig zag my bishop a little."

"Since you're pulling out all the stops, I may as well give up now!"

"I talked to Fereydoon yesterday," I told him.

"He's back?"

"As of two days ago."

"And?"

"I snuck him into the kitchen."

"Did you find out who Mehdi is?" Seyyed asked.

"Do you remember Taqi?"

"The one who . . ."

"Yeah," I said, "The one who left his rooms to me and went to America,"

"You know he . . ."

"Died?"

"He was killed," said Seyyed. "In a fight."

"I thought he'd gone to America!" I exclaimed.

"No, he was trying to get someone off his tail," replied Seyyed.

"Are you sure?"

"Ali said so."

"Did you know Mehdi was his alias?" I asked.

"How do you know?"

"The person calling from the US told me."

Seyyed leaned back: "All these games must be Kalantar's doing."

"I don't think so."

"What does this have to do with Prophet?"

"Apparently nothing," I said. "A case of the same name. A total accident. An untimely coincidence of two unrelated events. But it seems a mysterious hand must be at work here, engineering all these incidents to bring us to the brink of madness."

The waiter at Café de Phares set the coffee down on the table and his thin lips twisted into a mischievous smile. I dropped a sugar cube in the cup and started stirring the coffee: "Still, I think I've finally figured it all out."

"How do you mean?"

"Mehdi is none other than Fereydoon!" I said.

"Did he say so himself?"

"He did."

"Where did he disappear to?" Seyyed asked.

"He slipped away from his spiritual guide."

"I've never seen a disciple get away from his spiritual guide!" he said. "Where'd he go?"

"To the Netherlands."

Sipping his coffee, Seyyed asked, "Why the Netherlands?"

"He said Prophet had certain expectations of him that he couldn't fulfill."

"What expectations?"

"He didn't say."

"So that night when Prophet was screaming he wasn't gay . . ." Seyyed trailed off.

"No, it's something else."

"I hope he doesn't think we were talking behind his back?"

"Yesterday I went to Prophet's room for the second time," I said.

"Okay?"

"I told him, 'I was hoping we could make peace on the floor. Is my noise bothering you?' He said, 'No, there's just this one sex tape you play that bothers me.'"

"What tape?" asked Seyyed. "You don't even have a TV, let alone video tapes."

"Hey, there's a reason some people prefer radio over TV. When all you have is the sound, the imagination knows no bounds."

Seyyed set his empty coffee cup down on the table and sat back like he'd solved the riddle: "Ra'na must have been the one bothering him! Especially with that loud laugh of hers . . ."

"He admitted he heard everything. He said, 'I don't listen, it's sinful. But the walls are thin.'"

"Okay, what does this have to do with Mehdi?"

"Imagine someone came to live with us whose voice and mannerisms just so happened to be similar to those of a certain disciple who slipped out of the master's grasp . . ."

Seyyed leaned forward: "Did he say anything?"

"He said he heard Fereydoon's voice coming from inside my room!"

"So why did he hold the knife to my throat?"

I said nothing. There was no doubt Prophet had been confused and our pointless efforts were only going to be able to uncover the primary sources of his delusions, not the logic behind them.

Seyyed took two ten-franc coins out of his pocket and set them down on the table.

"Listen to me," he said. "You should think about finding another place to live too. He's completely off his rocker!"

I stared at him. The little vein over his left eye twitched. The waiter, who'd been standing in a corner, came over. He picked up the coins and smiled at Seyyed.

"Fereydoon said, 'If you want to help me, tell him I'm still on his path.'"

"Now there's two of them!" Seyyed said with a smirk.

I stood up, and as I was putting on my raincoat, said, "Something happened today that will either help him recover, or means we should expect more trouble."

"What happened?" asked Seyyed.

"When Prophet saw something was going on between Fereydoon and Bénédicte, he took the trowel right out of his disciple's hand and sent him off on some wild goose chase. As of today, it's Prophet who's helping Bénédicte!"

-12-

After Gabik's initial reconnaissance, it was Mathilde's turn to start the usual Q&A session from the top. When she asked what I needed, I lied and said, "I'm here to pay my rent," even though I just paid it a few days ago.

The landlord's wife was extremely forgetful, and old Érik François Schmidt always had to rummage through all his papers for an eternity to find the rent invoice, which he usually wrote out beforehand. Under such circumstances, saying what I just said could result in my paying rent for a second time that month, but it couldn't be helped. Considering the climate of dread and terror created by Prophet's attack, I could hardly say out loud right there in the hallway why I'd come. Especially since, after the day I went to see him, Prophet started leaving his door open, and our building was designed in such a way that if you stopped to listen, you could hear anyone talking in the stairwell.

Mathilde repeated the rest of her standard questions and eventually stepped aside to allow me to come into the entryway. Gabik, who'd wrestled his way out of Mathilde's arms, once again ran toward me and kept trying to get a rise out of me. No, this wouldn't do. I had to win him over, even if I had to flatter and spoil him. As I was about to call his name, however, a sudden doubt crept in. "What's this one called?"

"Gabik."

"Last time I thought his name was Ero."

"Ero died," she said.

"Gabik was dead before too!"

"Yes, this is Wolf."

They say forgetting is the body's natural defense against pain. They say the pain that a newborn experiences when it passes through that narrow birth canal is so intense, the child prefers to forget the pain of being born forever. As for me, the reason I was here was to finally free myself from a pain that had been plaguing me since Prophet arrived. The moment I needed to have all my wits about me—so that when Érik François Schmidt came, I wouldn't for the love of God look at his misshapen nose and forget why I was there—what was I thinking about? I was thinking about the day Mathilde's body decided to immediately erase everything that reached the gray matter in her brain. In that case, the future wouldn't turn out to be a delusion, nor would the past become a memory. Only the power of the moment would remain. That's it. How pleasant and yet unpleasant. It doesn't matter if this dog is Gabik or Bobby. It doesn't matter if I paid my rent or am paying it for a second time. If I had such a disease, I wouldn't hypothesize about the close relationship between disparate occurrences so much. I wouldn't discover the vast chasms in close relationships so often. I'd forget Bénédicte was sawing something yesterday too. I'd even forget she was sawing something a minute ago. I'd think she'd just picked up the saw. Right now. And the next moment would still be right now.

You can handle any kind of torture for a single moment. If just the moment ruled and nothing else, if "right now" was all there was, just "right now"—what secrets would no longer be buried in the heart of the earth! If only "right now" existed and not "later," no one would be anyone else's executioner. If only "right now" existed and not "later," Bénédicte, who now sawed all day long, would no longer be Bénédicte. Even if she herself said, "I'm Bénédicte," the next moment she wouldn't be.

It's the past that steals under your covers at night. When you roll over, you see it's right next to you. When you bury your head in your pillow, you realize the past is inside of it. The past is like a shadow, but even worse. When there's no light, shadows cease to exist. But the past is with you in the dark and in the silence. And I, who am incapable of bringing about my own demise, and who have been absolutely crucified by the harsh tyranny of the past, have no right to feel sorry for Mathilde. I, who am so unmoored my roots are flapping in the wind, don't blame this woman for not remembering that wet, foggy day in April 1943. That day when they singled out her first husband and a few others to take away, he turned around to say, "Mathilde, close the window when it gets windy. I'll get cold." She covers her tear-stained face with her hands, and as soon as she looks up, she sees a body writhing in the snow. Then, looking at her husband in shock, she sees the officer holding a rifle to his temple: "Say it!" The man opens his mouth, moaning like a whale, and blood spurts out of it, gushing all the way up to Mathilde's feet in a fountain. I don't blame her. I don't blame her.

Érik François Schmidt entered the foyer with a notebook in hand.

-13-

Everyone had dreams for the future except me. If Érik François Schmidt's dream was to make justice reign over this six-story building, Kalantar's dream was to make justice prevail over the sixth floor.

If Seyyed's dream was to own all the rooms on this floor one day and continue expanding his sphere of influence by knocking down the walls between them, Fereydoon's dream was to double the usable surface area of the rooms for the residents by adding a wooden loft.

If Prophet's dream was to have a disciple in each of the twelve rooms on the floor, I really had no dream, but now that I realized what I was running from had turned up right in my own backyard, I was slowly becoming enticed to play the role of Judah for this Prophet.

Seyyed still hadn't given up on his dream, even though he'd forfeited those two rooms for the time being and never set foot in them because he was afraid of Prophet (except on rare occasions—and even then, only when he knew I'd be there). Seyyed wasn't the type to play little games. He was setting things up so he could pull the rug out from under Kalantar, Fereydoon, and Prophet.

Prophet was making significant progress toward his dreams as well. Not only had he gotten his wayward pupil back on track, he'd added Bénédicte and Kalantar to his circle of followers too.

Kalantar, who used to come and go without making a sound, now stomped his feet as he came up the stairs, drunk on victory over his arch nemesis Seyyed, and walked down the sixth floor hall with enough swagger to remind even the walls to respect his authority. After putting a wooden loft in both his room and Bénédicte's,

Fereydoon was now expanding the usable floor space in Kalantar's room. All day long the din of the electric saw and sander enveloped the entire building in a deafening rumble. Every time the door opened or closed, the dirt and sawdust piled up outside poured into my room like a flowing sand dune, coating my carpets, sheets, and books in a thick layer of yellowy powder.

After Khatoun came to Paris, I began suffering from insomnia and smoked so much I started coughing constantly. Now I'd started coughing up bits of sawdust. I tried to console myself with the thought that the situation was temporary, but it was no use. It was true I'd turned down Fereydoon's kind offer and foregone the pleasure of having a wooden loft. It was true with Seyyed gone, the plans for building his loft had been abandoned. No matter how I calculated it, though, it seemed like it would be at least two months before the expansion of usable floor space was finished in the rest of the rooms. To make matters worse, although I could envision an end to the dirt, dust, and deafening rumble, there was no end in sight for the new misery that had been visited upon us. Now every time Fereydoon or Bénédicte rolled over in their lofts, the ancient boards (which had belonged to the gas company and were secretly looted from the alley as payback for plundering our great nation's oil reserves) groaned with a dry creak and destroyed the peace and quiet of our rudderless planet-ship.

Sometimes the woodwind harmony in the nighttime would embark on a never-ending performance. With every clack of Jean Jaurès's bed against the wall, or every slight noise I made, Fereydoon woke up and rolled over in his wooden loft. Every time Fereydoon tossed and turned, the boards groaned in protest and Bénédicte woke up. The call and response of the wood in Fereydoon and Bénédicte's rooms prompted people to open their doors to go to the bathroom. With the sound of doors opening and closing and people shuffling down the hallway, my chair would make a squeaking sound, Prophet's bed would bang against the wall, and once again the wood in Fereydoon and Bénédicte's rooms would creak.

All day long, I lay on my bed and listened to the noise outside, like a prisoner on death row who hears his wooden gallows being built. I couldn't go anywhere, since persistent insomnia had wiped me out, nor could I go to sleep. After Érik François Schmidt's angry yelling as he whipped Gabik, it was the doves' turn to sing "Off with his head." Then came the sound of Fereydoon's electric saw. Around ten the noise died down for a while and I passed out. But an hour later, loud knocking on the door woke me up. A strong male voice said something in French I didn't catch. I was sure it was the police. I opened the door. Two tall, tidy-looking men were at the door. One of them was holding a pamphlet with a picture of Jesus standing with sheep, the rest of which was hidden between the folds of his coat. The other one had a few books under his arm. Beating their way in with words, they advanced, their teeth whirring incessantly like coffee grinders. As soon as I realized they were Jehovah's Witnesses come to convert me, I tried to close the door. Four powerful hands pressed against it from the other side, their teeth-grinders churning away all the while. Terrified, I shoved the door closed like I was trying to escape from a wild bull, nodding toward Prophet's room as I yelled: "Jesus Christ is over there! Jesus Christ is over there!"

When the footsteps moved away from my door, my heart in my throat, I threw myself on the bed and pulled the covers over my head. A moment later they knocked on Prophet's door. I listened in. After all that, it was time for a bit of entertainment!

Unfortunately, Prophet didn't answer. As their footsteps echoed down the stairs, I noticed a letter had been slipped under my door. I opened the envelope:

> This wound will also heal, but I must say I have been utterly humiliated and feel betrayed. It never occurred to me that you would act so childishly after all the running around I did and after I stuck my neck out for you with so many different people. To tell you the truth, your behavior shows you have self-destructive tendencies!
>
> I wish to bring my letter to a close with this old proverb: God save me from the evil of my friends so that I might save myself from my enemies.
>
> Bernard

CHAPTER FOUR

Longing for a Lost Sea

-1-

I'm sitting on the edge of the bed. Immersed in darkness. I keep talking and talking. I talk so I won't get scared. Like someone shielding their face with their arms in the dark. This is the only thread connecting me and the shadow. For twenty-six long years I lugged it around. I would take on the form of any idiot I came across, from movie stars to the neighborhood shopkeeper. I was terrified of daylight. I was terrified the sunlight daggers might shine on the crown of my head. I was terrified I'd lose focus for a moment and the shadow would drag itself out from under my toenails. In the morning when I went to sleep, I'd leave the light on, shining at an angle so it'd always be beside me, on the wall opposite. I knew the damage it was inflicting on me would be my downfall in the end. I hadn't slept for weeks now. The pungent smell of fried onions, plus the sawdust and plaster, made it hard for me to breathe. My lungs felt tight.

Two days ago M.A.R. came to see me, totally out of the blue. She was the only one who could save me. So, I did something to push her away forever: "What are you doing here?" I asked. "After all these years?"

"After fifteen years."

"Right, right. Fifteen years."

"I've been wanting to come for six years," she explained, "but they stopped me every time."

"I didn't ask why you're so late."

"I came to see you."

"Great, you've seen me. Drowning in shit. Why don't you leave?"

"I have to help you. You're destroying yourself."

"No, someone else is destroying me," I said.

"It's possible to live alone while surrounded by other people, you know."

"As it happens, it's other people who are living in the middle of my solitude."

"It's your solitude that's forced people to step in."

"Did you come here to lecture me?"

"I came to help," she said.

"Everybody's helping me!" I snapped. "One's receiving revelations, another wants to double my usable floor space. Somebody else shows up unannounced out of the blue. If you want to help me, go away. Go away and leave me in peace!"

She left. She closed the door halfway and left. I wished she'd come back. What an idiot! Now who was going to deal with my dead body?

She came back. She returned as calmly as she had left. Half an hour later, when she rolled up her sleeves to restore order to the chaos that was my apartment, I picked up the kitchen knife and screamed at her that if she didn't go, I'd kill her.

What an idiot! She'd gone to such lengths to find me and then I . . .

"When I finally tracked you down," she said. "I didn't hesitate. I slept outside embassies night after night and didn't get discouraged by rejections. It didn't matter what country gave me a visa."

She knew Europe like the back of her hand. She knew it was all connected by land and that wherever there was a sliver of waterfront, there were boats. Boats so big that you could think of them as moving pieces of land. As soon as the Austrian consul recalled that night at the Italian diplomat's house where she sat in the courtyard fountain, legs bare, singing like a nymph in the depths of a long-lost sea, he stamped her passport with no hesitation.

Now that she was throwing me off a cliff, it was like she wanted to make sure I didn't hit any rocks on the way down. She picked up a white card and wrote a phone number on it. She held it out to me along with the passport: "I'm going to Vienna for the next two weeks on vacation. If anything comes up, you can call me."

She'd tried to leave Austria a few times, but every time they stopped her at the border. She was stuck there for a few years until she was able to find a way out.

"I married Heinrich," she said. "I had no other choice. I had to get a hold of a passport, whatever it took."

She'd crossed into Italy on foot. Finally, she stowed away on a boat. She slipped into the cargo hold between some animal cages. The boat was headed to Barcelona, but she couldn't cross the border there either. Finally, she trekked on foot for two months through the snow and cold of the Pyrenees to make it to this side.

"I had no choice but to spend the night at the summit," she told me. "There was snow everywhere. In the cold and dark, I managed to collect a few branches and started a fire between two larger rocks.

Once the fire got going, I realized there was a snake curled up next to me. I didn't want to die without seeing you. I said, 'A flute is no match for me!' and started singing. It bared its fangs. I kept singing. Its eyelids grew heavy. My voice could charm the snake, but never you!"

After I brandished the knife, she left. She watched me the whole time she went down the stairs. She didn't scold me or get upset. She looked at me and left.

-2-

All last night, the wind raged. My room was like a piece of driftwood in a storm. I very clearly heard the building's wooden skeleton groan as it shifted. Bénédicte's cat wouldn't stop meowing. Every once in a while, the sound of things falling or breaking, accompanied by the howling wind, etched itself into the night. I got up a few times to close the window, but every time, some unknown poet's words convinced me not to:

> Let the wind come.
> Let it sweep away this room, these pages
> Let me slip into the night
> Through this window,
> A lifeless orifice in the wall—
>
> Let me revolve with the legion of frozen stars . . .

The wind rose up in waves like a furious sea and slammed into the walls as the sound of things falling and breaking continued. I kept thinking the wind would rip out my window and the exposed glass would slice some unlucky pedestrian's head off. The bloody pane of glass would shatter into a thousand pieces on the asphalt, and the pedestrian's severed head would roll up to the door of the bakery. Just imagining the scene, I started shaking so much I popped up and moved toward the window without realizing it. It seemed this move was a natural extension of the trembling—like the ripples around a stone dropped in a pond, its rings radiated out from my inner terror to collide with the base of the window.

The window was a metal rectangle that had been awkwardly covered with glass and, like most attic windows, opened vertically. It moved up toward the sky to open and came down toward the ground to close. The latch on the frame was metal and had three holes spaced equally apart. Depending on which hole you chose, you could prop the window open at different angles. The window in my room was on the middle option. When I touched the latch, a horrible thought crossed my mind. As always, as soon as I became afraid of something, that's exactly what would happen. This time, too, as soon as I pulled the hook out, the horror I'd imagined became a reality: Rising up at that very moment, a formidable wind pushed me back, tore the window clean off with the hinges, and whisked it away, spinning through the air like a piece of paper. It was almost as if the hook wasn't there to latch the window, but to trigger that fateful event.

I stood motionless, awaiting the sound of a terrible crash. The unlucky pedestrian, a drunk homeless man, was staggering closer through the wind. The window whirled through the air, the edge of the glass pane sticking out of the frame. A thousand times the doomed man's head was separated from his body; a thousand times the sound of the window shattering into a thousand pieces reverberated in my mind. But outside, there was only the sound of wind. Not a shattering sound, or even the sound of an impact. Even Bénédicte's cat, which had been crying up until a moment ago, was quiet now. Bewildered, I stood there in the middle of the room. It seemed the window wasn't made of glass and metal at all; it was a piece of silk caught in the wind. In shock, I edged closer to the window frame. It was a pit of darkness, the toothless mouth of a monster. I went to stick my head out to see if I could see anything, but a dreadful thought made me suddenly pull back: what if the window is out there, like a spinning blade, waiting for me to stick my head out in curiosity? And then . . .

Is it possible the idea for the guillotine was conceived of on a night like this? If curiosity got the best of me, what would the papers say tomorrow? "In terms of worldly pleasures, he did not share the same fortune as King Louis XVI, but in death . . ."

I got back into bed, still listening carefully, and thought about what Prophet had said. My bed belonged to Satan, and unfortunate events awaited me in the future!

What event could be more unfortunate than the wind whisking your window away and you having no idea where it went?

To what extent are we responsible for our own actions? I went to close my window, but a storm came just at the wrong moment to rip it off the wall and carry it away. Now my window has its own distinct fate. Maybe instead of decapitating the poor pedestrian, it'll just break his leg or let him off easy with some kind of flesh wound. That doesn't mean that action's existence ends there, though. Say the window lands somewhere there are no pedestrians. The startling sound of the glass shattering on the asphalt will reverberate and continue its forward motion in several directions:

Kalantar's wife, who's become dreadfully thin, takes a Lysanxia pill and goes to bed. Lately Bénédicte started pounding on their door, over and over again, late at night: "All that racket's keeping me up!" And every time Kalantar's wife swore on her life she hadn't made a sound and Bénédicte was imagining things.

Just a few minutes ago, Bénédicte banged on the door and yelled at her, "You slackers might not have jobs but some of us have to get up at four in the morning and go to work!"

She was telling the truth. She did get up at 4:00 AM, but she went to work at eight. And then, when Bénédicte added, "Who washes dishes at midnight, by the way?" Kalantar's wife loses it and goes after her. Bénédicte flees to her room and locks the door behind her. Right at that moment, Fereydoon shows up: "What's wrong?"

"I'm losing my mind," Kalantar's wife says, breaking into tears. "I'm sitting there quietly reading French, and she says I woke her up by washing dishes!"

Just then Fereydoon says something he imagines will calm her down, but it's like throwing fuel on the fire, and she's now aflame from head to toe!

She takes another pill, planning to sleep until Kalantar gets home in the morning from the night shift. A little later comes the horrible sound of the window smashing into the asphalt. It's just the wake-up call Kalantar's wife needs to realize not every noise bothers Bénédicte. In that instant, she recalls what Fereydoon said and comes to a strange decision.

For the moment, it does not concern us whether the outward ripple of this event peters out into a mild breeze or swells into a storm in Chicago.

A little farther down the street, Jean is making love to Emmanuelle. Emmanuelle's indifference has been causing problems for a while now for Jean, who's a shy and insecure young man, which means he's had to come up with an excuse every time for his inability to perform. Emmanuelle acting like it doesn't matter provides Jean no comfort at all. In fact, it fans the flames of his insecurity and mistrust, especially since Emmanuelle hasn't bothered to turn on the gramophone in a long time.

At his wit's end with the whole situation, Jean is giving himself a final chance. He gets a good night's sleep the night before; he takes a cold shower before coming over; he eats a light meal and immediately takes two Carboslim pills, so a bloated stomach doesn't break his concentration in the middle of everything; and for the first time, he's the one to turn on the gramophone.

Despite the storm rattling the building, everything is going Jean's way to the lyrics of *Carmen*. For the first time in ages, he manages to elicit the sound of Emmanuelle expressing her passion, though not with as much intensity as before. *Carmen* pushes her voice to the limit. "Higher, higher, higher, la-la-la, la-ha-ha-ha-ha, la-la-la, la-ha-ha-ha-ha." But just when Jean's tears of passion are about to brim over, a bizarre crash of metal and glass disrupts everything.

Even if Emmanuelle hadn't been determined to tell Jean the truth that night, my small action—closing the window—wouldn't have led to this.

Outside it was silent. The storm had subsided, but there was no sign of my fallen window. I'd come to accept the fact that it wasn't a sheet of glass and metal; it was a piece of silk that was gone with the wind. Nothing prevented me from ruminating on the consequences of that, however. The movement of something as delicate as silk could also bring about the same catastrophe as the flapping of a butterfly's wings:

Imagine you ask a woman on the street for the time. She pauses. She looks at her watch: "It's 5:10."

For you, asking this question is an action that's over and done with. But the action itself, like a newly-spawned monster, continues its existence independent of you. Just those few seconds are enough to make the woman, who hurries into the subway station, miss her train. Two minutes later, another train arrives and she gets on. Several stations down the line, there's a horrific crash with an oncoming train, leading to the deaths of several passengers. If not for your simple action, the woman could have gotten on an earlier train. But now she will have her name added to the list of victims.

No doubt this seems to you an absurd hypothetical scenario that could only be imagined by a mind afflicted with paranoia.

And yet, even if someone doesn't believe in that absurd hypothetical scenario, when he sees the news about the collision of two trains in Gare du Nord, he can't help but think that, had he not been standing directly opposite the entrance to the Oberkampf metro station last year on the afternoon of April 13th at 5:20 p.m., the woman he asked for the time wouldn't have died as a result of his action.

With that woman's death, a man, who had for some time been standing near the end of a death loop, was pushed one step closer to the brink.

-3-

I'd been hoping Faust and his partner would do anything they wanted with me, except send me back to that shithole. What would I even do if I did go back? There was nobody left. My wife had been killed in a train crash, and my daughter, who started believing all kinds of strange things and thought the end times were nigh, vanished one day. Then, after I'd searched for her everywhere, the police concluded she was one of the as-yet unidentified victims of the Order of the Solar Temple, since they'd found a picture of Dr. Luc Jouret, the cult leader, in the pages of one of her school books. Only Khatoun was left, who I'd sent to a retirement home. If I went back now, I'd have to go see her every week and hear her complain: "Save me from these unbelievers! They keep feeding me meat that isn't *halal*. How will I answer to God?"

I'd told her that this place was especially for elderly Muslim clients. Now that she'd found everything out, though, how could I convince her?

No, I wasn't up for going back to the shithole called the real world. I turned toward the invisible partner in exasperation, "You know who plunged the knife into my back!"

The partner placed a wooden chair in the pillar of light and now with his legs crossed, took a deep drag of his pipe: "Yes, but who provoked him to do it?"

The smoke was trailing downwards from his pipe. That very fact was enough to convince me that I was truly dead and was now in the heavens above. So, for the first time, I decided to answer everything with the utmost honesty.

"You have the unadulterated version at your disposal," I said. "You can cross-check it against everything I'm telling you."

The Native American opened a stack of papers that contained the unadulterated version of the narrative, with the Toshiba logo at the top. "You wrote: 'Seyyed had realized words were worthless. That's why he expended them so generously. He also recognized something else: The spiritual void in people, and their almost pathological need to hear nice things and compliments they didn't deserve. The night Ra'na suggested she type Seyyed's work, the thin vein over his left eye twitched. He paused and said, "It's just a few pages, I'll type it up myself." He said this as he was leaving, but immediately regretted it, and stayed another half an hour so he could take her up on it by saying, "So, did you really mean it?" and bring her with him. He needed that window of time to make all his calculations and determine whether letting her do it would set him back or not. And if he did offer, would she be able to play it off somehow like she'd done him a favor? (Like that night at a party when Jessica, an American girl, asked him where he was from and he said, "Qom," but he pronounced it in a way that made me think, as I observed this conversation, that he definitely meant Qom, Iran—the little desert city where he was born—whereas Jessica, who didn't even know where Iran was on the world map, thought he meant Rome. And then, when Jessica animatedly started to recount the beauty and grandeur of Rome's historical buildings, Seyyed was so engaged in the conversation, she thought a proud Italian was praising her knowledge of geography, while I was thinking this gentle young man didn't have the heart to burst someone's bubble, even about something so trivial.)

'Yes, Seyyed had to calculate which was better to lose—me or Ra'na—if he were forced to give one of us up. (Seyyed had found some use even for me; he needed someone experienced to look over the silly little songs he wrote once in a while and fix them up.) Seyyed's math was right. But despite all his cleverness, there was one thing he hadn't accounted for: that the walls in this place were thinner than paper, and in the room right next to mine lived someone who was still kicking himself over one question. When he found his wife in bed with that European scumbag, why did he leave it up to God and not rip the guy's head off? The affirmative answer that Seyyed gave Ra'na was a simple auditory vibration created by his teeth and lips, and a few days later, the continuation of its independent movement transformed into a knife. Its threatening tip was destined for Seyyed's throat, while its piercing blade was destined to stab me shortly thereafter.'"

The invisible partner cleared his throat, "So, in this supposedly unadulterated version, you had poor Seyyed take the blame for everything!"

"Look Mister . . . Partner, it's true the night Seyyed took Ra'na up on her suggestion, he knew things were already rough between me and her. The trap he laid out for her, though, was way more subtle than that. He knew the best method for picking up women was no method at all. He'd learned from experience women go crazy for a guy who serves them a handsome face while pretending he's completely unfazed. Especially if he lets a few things slip in conversation that make her feel like she has access to the innermost secrets of his soul. Meanwhile, Seyyed did have access to the innermost secrets of her soul! It wasn't so simple as all that, though. In reality, it was a complex game where everyone was both hunter and hunted. Ra'na, who'd witnessed my fickle personality and selfish behavior, was thinking if the only thing she was going to get out of a relationship was limited dining and sleeping privileges, why not at least start a relationship with someone who provided her with more? Seyyed's rooms were connected and felt more spacious. This, plus the hot shower that he had installed, raised Seyyed's rooms to the level of a small apartment which no longer fit the bill of an 'attic room.' Most days he ate out, too.

"When Seyyed brought Ra'na over to his rooms, he thought he'd lured her in, but what he didn't know was that two days earlier, Ra'na had asked me, not understanding the extravagances of Seyyed's lifestyle: 'How does he live?'

"I responded, using the same phrase Seyyed had said himself: 'The carpet gallery!' Her eyes grew round and a lightbulb went off in her head. The next day, this lightbulb—in its natural progression—took the shape of refusing to sleep with me. The day after that, it led to the suggestion that she type Seyyed's stories, and a few days later, to the tip of Prophet's knife."

The partner took a deep puff of his pipe: "So, you found two accomplices in this whole thing to assist you in the murder! You don't seriously want me to believe you were just a victim in all this?

"Look, I don't know if your partner is here right now or—"

"He went somewhere. He'll be back."

I was worried. Taking advantage of the rapport that had developed between me and the partner, I asked, "Where'd he go?"

"He forgot his pills and went to go get them."

"What pills?"

"Lysanxia. So, you were saying."

"Look Mr . . . Ugh, God damn this stupid habit . . ."

"It doesn't matter. Either one is fine."

"Yes, Mr . . . Partner . . . I tried so hard to follow that older gentleman's advice. But my being in love couldn't last. After a week, either I was disappointed or they were. Plus, I don't know how to say this but . . . one of my body parts doesn't work."

"It's because of the Lysanxia!"

This was Faust's voice reverberating in the air. Tapping his pipe, the partner reclaimed his spot on the left.

"They said it was because of living in exile," I told them. "They said it was all in my head. When the brain is incapacitated, the body doesn't do its job right either. I thought maybe M.A.R. had cast a spell on me."

"No, it's because of the Lysanxia!"

I was about to say, "Aren't you afraid the company that makes it will sue you?" but my tongue got tied and I said, "Aren't you afraid? Do you take it?"

"I'm not married. Besides, it works. Why do you think Seyyed takes it by the handful?"

"He had a heart problem."

"You're so naive!"

"Why did he take it then?"

"Keep reading."

". . . Ra'na, like every other woman," I read aloud, "was an innocent bystander whose existence tormented me, for no other reason than that whenever I went to see her, I was looking for someone else—a girl who'd been lost in the river. So, in one sense, her presence was just a headache for me. When I saw both she and Seyyed were dreaming about other people, I told myself the only solution was to bring them together."

Faust, who was now sitting in the partner's spot, said, "And you set your plan into motion!"

"Actually, I didn't have a particular plan," I told him. "I just had to help them carry out their own plans. Seyyed wanted all the information he could get his hands on, and I gave him more than he needed, so much that Ra'na would feel he had access to the innermost secrets of her soul. Then, to convince Seyyed that me and Ra'na were definitely over, I set up our meeting at Ingrid's concert on purpose. If Ra'na decided not to sleep with me anymore, it was because she was hoping to pave the way for a relationship with Seyyed. By letting him know we were through, I very quickly paved the way for her. That day in the kitchen when I offered her my help, I knew she was mostly suffering from a lack of human contact, not missing Seyyed. When Seyyed left and the floor emptied out, it was an opportunity for her to mull over everything that happened and recognize her mistakes. Instead of seizing the opportunity, though, I tried to convince her she was struggling because she missed Seyyed. Then I set everything up so the two of them would end up together."

"Don't give yourself too much credit. Do you know what happened between Ra'na and Seyyed on the night of the attack, when she went to walk him to Agnès's house?"

"No, I don't."

"Did you believe the story about Prophet camping out outside Ra'na's room?"

"You mean it wasn't true?"

"If you recall, Seyyed put a few Lysanxia pills in his mouth before setting out."

"Right, well, his heart was acting up again," I said.

"No! Seyyed made up that story about the heart attack to convince his wife, or whoever else he needed to, that he didn't have long to live."

"What would he gain by doing that?"

"What would he gain?" Murnau's Faust smirked. Then, imitating Agnès, he continued: "Oh dear . . . Such a sweet young man! It's such a shame he doesn't have long to live. Well, seeing as that's the case, I better not to get in the way of him enjoying his life!"

"You mean, it was all for show?" I asked.

"You're saying you didn't know?"

"Well, he may have taken advantage of it sometimes, when circumstances required. But why did he take Lysanxia, then?"

"Why did you?"

"At first, for depression. Then, once I realized its other effects, I took it when I had important meetings."

"For him, all meetings were important," Faust explained. "So he took it every day. By the handful."

"So that means he also . . ."

"For him, just one thing was important: the magnetism of his existence!"

Faust was right. I remembered the day Seyyed left his day planner behind and I, the double-crossing and curious type, started snooping. (In my defense, Seyyed, sweet young man that he was, had given me his spare key so I wouldn't have to go to the pool or the sauna for a shower, like lots of other people did.) On one page he'd copied out a quote from the book *Satan and Another*, by Reza Sigamesh:

> Inside every person is a child that lives with him to the end of his days. For that child to show itself, all we have to do is ward off the lines and wrinkles that time etches on our faces, so we can outrun it. This is the only way not to get intimidated by someone, no matter how much more important they are than us. Or, if you like, this is the only

way to intimidate someone else. In a word, it means "the magnetism of existence!"

Underneath that, Seyyed had added, "Lines and wrinkles on your face are a dead giveaway! You have to find a way to replace your face with a mask . . ." And on the next line, he'd added hurriedly: "Lysanxia! Lysanxia!"

Alarmed by the breadth of Faust and the partner's knowledge of events, and pleased by my logical decision to confess everything, I brought up something else that was worrying me now: "You keep using past tense. Did something happen to him?"

"He didn't have long to live!"

"So he wasn't lying."

Faust stared into the distance: "He became so obsessed with the idea, it really came to pass." Then, imitating Seyyed, he added, "To die young makes life fulfilling!"

"What did he die of?"

"A heart attack!"

-4-

My eyes were just closing when I was woken up by a woman screaming: "Come down! Come down! Please, I'm begging you!"

That morning, moments after Érik François Schmidt's shouting and Gabik's pitiful howls, the turtle doves returned. The night before, the wind stripped the window off my roof, and the turtle doves, squawking more intensely and feverishly than ever before, flooded in through the hole where the window used to be. Walking all over the desk and books, they screeched at the top of their lungs, "Off with his head! Off with his head!" A few were perched on the edge of the easel, and another was on the arm of the old wooden chair next to the door, screaming with all its force: "Off with his head! Off with his head!"

Once I realized what they were saying to the rhythm of that ominous tune, I couldn't stand the sound of it. At first I said to myself: "You're being paranoid—don't get carried away!" I tried to interpret it as something other than: "Off with his head!" I managed to convince myself initially they were saying "Up out of bed!" but I quickly abandoned that, since the syllables didn't fit the rhythm, plus it made it even harder for me to sleep. Then, looking for a phrase that would work, I came up with, "Creation is bred!" That didn't really fit the rhythm either, though. Feeling hopeless again, I decided they could only be saying that menacing phrase I heard at first. Now that they were right above my head, they were squawking so loud a phrase finally occurred to me that both fit the rhythm and didn't have an irritating meaning: "Go on ahead! Go on ahead!" Still sleep eluded me, though, since I kept asking myself: "Go on ahead with what?"

After the turtle doves left, I slowly peeked my head out from under the covers. The table, the books—the whole room was caked with bird poop. Then, up on the row of dusty books, I spotted an old turtle dove still sitting there, trembling, its head nestled in its feathers. Something had fallen on the floor next to the chair, which I hadn't paid any attention to while I was hovering between sleep and consciousness. And now that strange sound . . . Today of all days, when it was finally dead silent in the hallway for the first time in ages!

"Come down! Please come down!"

I thought it was Emmanuelle, but there was no hint of pleasure in those screams. I wanted to go do a little reconnaissance, but my chronic insomnia had sapped any energy I had to get out of bed. I pulled the blanket firmly over my head. But the continued repetition of the word "down" piqued my curiosity.

"Come down, come down. I said come down, God dammit!"

As I lie there under the covers, I tried to guess what it was all about just from those few shouted words. But the voice was a stranger's, the words few, and my imagination, limitless.

I got up. The pressure in my bladder had been building for a while. When I got to the bathroom, I froze. The screams were coming from inside! Stranger still—my window, which the wind had blown away the night before, was now on the ground in front of the bathroom, next to the wall. Confused and disoriented, I went back to my room.

The cries then took on a bizarre, pleading tone: "Please. Please!"

The sounds sent me back to many years ago, to the empty courtyard of an old house. To a bathroom in the corner of the courtyard. To a girl who locked herself in there with some crochet needles. To a young friend who sat next to me, covered in sweat, and with every one of the girl's screams, clutched my arm and sobbed. "It's so horrible! It's so horrible."

"Come down. Please! I'm begging you. I give you my word."

The addition of a new phrase to the sequence snapped me out of that awful memory. Plus, the pressure on my bladder, which was increasing by the moment, forced me (who avoids interfering in other people's lives) to head back toward the bathroom, frustrated and on edge. The door was still closed and the screams kept coming: "Forgive me! I promise you. Come down. Please!"

With each additional word, the face of whoever the woman was screaming at took on a new shape in my mind. I thought of the super and his wife. I'd walked in on them a few times in the bathroom on my floor. The fact that they were both in there, along with their history of addiction and several other signs, left no room for doubt that their coming to the bathroom was somehow or another related to doing drugs.

Doing drugs was their business, but using the bathroom on this floor was my business too, especially now that the pressure on my bladder had become intolerable. Besides, they had a private bathroom in their apartment on the ground floor. I put my ear up to the door: "Who's there?"

"Come down, please!"

I came out of the bathroom foyer and looked around. Emmanuelle's door was slightly ajar. A shiver of fear went through me. I couldn't imagine these screams were coming from that girl who normally walked by so slowly and whispered hello. I tapped lightly on the door to her room. A loud scream prompted me to rush back to the bathroom and try the handle.

The door wouldn't open. There was something in the way. I shoved the door with my shoulder. In the tiny gap that appeared, I saw a woman with her back to me, clinging to someone's foot, as the rest of their body hung out the window.

CHAPTER FIVE

Handknit Socks, Made in Iran

-1-

Érik François Schmidt wiggled his toes in the thick, fluffy knit socks Seyyed had brought him from Iran as a souvenir. He picked up the book lying on the table and opened it to page 171, which he'd bookmarked with one of Milosh's unpaid rent notices.

Mathilde returned from the kitchen with a bottle of wine and filled Érik François Schmidt's glass. As she went to sit down, she fixed her startled eyes on him and asked, with a voice that held some unearthly sweetness in it, "What's so great about this book you can't put it down?"

Érik François Schmidt hadn't been able to fall asleep last night, no matter how much he tossed and turned. Kalantar's words were poking his brain like a thorn, tormenting him. Just before Kalantar showed up, Seyyed had dropped by again with his tape recorder.

"The problem with the French," said Seyyed, "is they don't value their national heroes enough. And yet, the same people are prepared to admit their heroes' mistakes whenever necessary." Then he added that he'd be coming next week with one of France's top photographers so Érik François Schmidt could get his picture taken.

For the past two months or so, Seyyed had been stopping by once or twice a week to record Érik François Schmidt's memoirs. At first, Érik François Schmidt said no.

"Wherever the pulse of Europe was beating," Seyyed told him, "you were there: thc Spanish Civil War, the Resistance Army, the Nazi concentration camps . . . And then there's your private life! You lost your first wife in the concentration camp, and your wife lost her first husband the same way. Most significant is the work that you've begun with this building. But even your closest friends don't seem to appreciate you properly! None of them have approached you to do an interview?"

"No, they've just published my essays once or twice. In any case, it's not like I've done anything important."

"Don't be modest! You're the living embodiment of the history of France!"

The afternoons were made up of lethal, stupefying hours. That's why Érik François Schmidt's happiest days were when Seyyed came to take down his memoirs.

Half an hour after Seyyed left, Kalantar came to settle up. As he handed over his key, he said, "I'm on my way out, but just so you know, that guy totally pulled a fast one on you."

Érik François Schmidt was taken aback. "I don't understand what you mean."

Kalantar reached into his bag and pulled out my book, which had been published in a fancy edition, and laid it on the table. "Read this book and you'll get it!"

Érik François Schmidt figured he'd start reading the book the next day, but that night when he went to bed, he kept turning what

Kalantar said over in his mind. He got up again, went back to the guest room and started reading it that evening. He read straight through until morning. In the morning, he dozed off for a few hours and then took it up again first thing, without even eating breakfast.

Again Mathilde asked, "What's so great about this book you can't put it down?"

Accustomed to Mathilde's forgetfulness by now, Érik François Schmidt scratched the growth on the right side of his nose, which was now the size of an apple, and gave Mathilde a smile that she didn't understand.

"The woodwind harmony in the nighttime," he replied.

Mathilde, who comprehended nothing of this response, asked with surprise, "Is it about music?"

Though Érik François Schmidt had already reached eighty-nine years of age, his mind was remarkably sharp, and he generally avoided using sentences that were too critical like, "As I told you before . . . ," as much as he could, so he didn't hurt Mathilde's feelings. Plus, since he was hard of hearing, he often didn't hear what Mathilde was saying and so couldn't be sure if she was repeating the same questions or not. If he didn't ask her to repeat herself, it was because asking was as good as saying, "Did you forget I was hard of hearing?" And that would hurt his own feelings. So he tried to guess what she said. If his guess turned out to be wrong, it didn't matter, since Mathilde would forget what she'd said anyway.

Now this was probably the tenth time Érik François Schmidt had answered the same question that morning, or maybe, it was the tenth time he thought Mathilde was asking the same question. But he still marked the page in his book with his finger and scratched the large growth on the right side of his nose: "Do you remember the skinny fellow with the crooked nose? The one on the top floor?"

Érik François Schmidt was so eager to keep reading his book he slipped up and made a mistake that was most unusual for him—"Do you remember . . . ?" So harsh! Both to cover up his mistake and speed things along, he immediately added, "He published a memoir of his time living here."

"Who?"

"The top floor guy."

"The top floor of what?"

"He was forty years old, Iranian."

"What was his name?"

Érik François Schmidt thought it would be rather unpleasant to bring up the murder that had happened in the building's stairwell, so to change the subject he said, "I only have a few pages left. I'll tell you all about it when I'm done."

Mathilde got up and kissed him on the forehead. "I'm going to bed," she said. "Goodnight."

Érik François Schmidt adjusted his gold-frame glasses, which had been broken for a long time and tied in the back with a piece of twine. "Goodnight."

Mathilde hadn't yet left the room when Érik François Schmidt called to her: "Mathilde."

"What is it?"

He wiggled his toes in his socks again. "Mathilde."

"Do you need something?"

"It's cold out tonight. Take care," he told her, opening his book.

•

The super's wife had blond hair, and the woman I'd seen from behind had hair the same color as Emmanuelle's.

I hated myself for interfering in other people's lives. I turned around and went back. When I stopped in front of the door to the room, my legs felt weak.

The fact that the French normally didn't interfere in anyone else's business was a huge selling point for me, committed as I was to my own isolation. But for the first time I asked myself—where was the limit to this non-intervention? And how beneficial was this hands-off approach, really?

I was at a loss for what to do. If this was just a romance drama that needed a climax to reach a resolution, all my interference could do is disrupt their lives. But what if someone's life was at stake?

To be honest, my problem wasn't a philosophical one. My bladder was aching, and the chronic insomnia was killing me. Besides, if a person couldn't face carrying on with their life, that was their problem. If, on the other hand, they just wanted to force their problems to a dramatic climax and my presence encourages them to make that climax happen, why should I let my conscience torture me for intervening and disrupt the tiny bit of sleep I was able to get?

When Bénédicte opened her door, it was like opening the door to all my problems. She gave me a brief glance, then craned to look down to the end of the hall. We could still hear the woman's screams, now accompanied by constant sobs: "Forgive me! Forgive me!"

Bénédicte threw me a nasty, disapproving look and slammed her door shut.

Well, my predicament had been resolved. The French preferred not to intervene in other people's affairs, even in cases like this. My conscience clear, I went back to my room and shut the door.

"Come down! Come down!"

I couldn't sleep or go relieve myself. I was at the end of my rope. I opened the door. Bénédicte's door opened at the exact same moment. She threw me another quick look and popped her head out to look down the hall. Then she glanced at me again as she closed the door. This time, however, her look held no rebuke in it, and she even hesitated for a moment.

Who could believe it? Up to this point, Bénédicte had used any excuse to knock on my door, and now she was letting this golden opportunity slip by. Maybe she was afraid of hurting Prophet's feelings?

For the first time ever, I went and knocked on her door. Cautiously, she opened it slightly.

"Somebody's about to throw themselves out the window! I think it's Milosh."

I'm not sure why I said something so stupid. Milosh was gay, after all. It did the trick, though, and these were perhaps the only words that could have moved Bénédicte to action. At the end of the day, Milosh was the only one Bénédicte was on halfway-decent terms with. Whenever she went travelling, Milosh would water her plants and watch her cat.

Bénédicte ran full speed to the bathroom.

"Milosh! Milosh!"

I couldn't believe that this woman—who was running anxiously toward the bathroom and calling out to Milosh in a voice trembling with emotion—was the same woman who always issued orders like a drill sergeant in her newsletters and would pick fights with just about anyone, on any occasion.

Suddenly there was a loud scream from the bathroom. Bénédicte rushed out of the small foyer and begged me to help. Terrified, I edged forward. The bathroom door was open. The woman, still clinging to the man's leg, turned to look at me. It was Emmanuelle! Her eyes were red from so much crying.

Bénédicte plunged forward decisively: "Come help!"

Emmanuelle was still shrieking. Before Bénédicte had even touched his leg, the man slowly brought his head back in through the window: "Get the fuck out of here." He said it with such conviction and calm, you'd think he'd gone up there to repair something, not kill himself.

I, who was standing behind Bénédicte, very naturally got the fuck out of there right away. It was obvious I was just in the way. Plus, I'd made another horrific mistake. It was Jean up there, not Milosh! Even worse, it looked like I'd dragged Bénédicte, who had no intention of intervening, out of her room on purpose just so she could get cursed at.

I went straight back to my room. As I shut my door, I saw Bénédicte shutting hers too. Our eyes met for a moment, and every expletive in the entire world was hurled my way by the thunderbolt of her wounded, furious look.

•

Back when I used to act (another one of my dead-end careers), I once delivered a line very mechanically. I couldn't spark my imagination even when I got critique after critique. The director—a tyrannical, grouchy man called Ghassemi—sent me up on the stage under the glare of a bright light and said: "Keep repeating that line until I tell you to stop." For the first few minutes, I repeated the line the same way, but he never told me to stop. Eventually I got tired of it and tried to change up the rhythm or the tone so I could convey something more than the exact words: "I don't know what you're trying to do here. I've had enough. Can you please stop so I can get out of this dead-end loop." He didn't tell me to stop, though, and I was getting more and more frustrated. Through those same words, I tried to convey something else: "That's enough, alright? I'm talking myself hoarse. What do these tyrannical orders have to do with theater?"

He still didn't tell me to stop. This time I said something else through the same words, "Please! I'm begging you."

I was really exhausted and delivered the last lines with a slack jaw, but he didn't back down. Once I realized his heart was made of stone and his head of chalk, I blew up and said, through the same words, "Let me come down from here, you asshole! Things are getting way out of hand. This is ridiculous. That's enough! Prick." Then I fell silent. The next moment, I added, pleading through those same words. "Please. Please."

Finally the moment arrived when, tired and drained, I asked myself: "What was the point of the director's eccentric behavior?" Then I realized I'd twisted and contorted that line, which I kept delivering in the same monotonous way, into a thousand and one different shapes. This was his goal all along—to bring me to this point. I started the line again, and this time delivered it with gratitude, singing it in an exhilarated tone, "Forgive me! Forgive me!"

If all human feelings can be conveyed through a few words, then what did humanity invent all this vocabulary for? To better convey their meaning? Why didn't Emmanuelle convey her meaning more clearly, then? If primitive men had only a few words at their disposal to express their point, does that mean we have more complex emotions than them? Why did Emmanuelle use just a few words?

Now Emmanuelle had incorporated the element of rage into her new performance of those few choice words. Suddenly she brought her voice to a crescendo and screamed as though it were her last try: "Come down from there!" Then her voice lowered again and took on a pleading tone, "Please." Then contrition: "Forgive me." Then promises and deception: "I promise you." A moment later, the order of the tones switched. A few words were dropped, others were given more emphasis. What was important was not the variation in the words, but the different states Emmanuelle's mind was passing through and the different formations in which they were expressed. Imagine what meanings lay behind these words that Emmanuelle was leaving unexpressed!

There were things she expressed that I didn't understand, and things she held back that Jean didn't understand.

"Please, please."

My bladder was about to explode. I grabbed a teacup and went over to the window. There was nothing else to be done. Luckily, there was no sign of the woman who lived in the building across the street and was constantly examining her armpits in the mirror. I dumped my cup out the window, but it felt like my bladder had grown as big as my whole body. I filled and emptied it a few more times before I could stretch out on the bed without any worries. Just at that moment, however, some sounds erupted from the hallway that let me know the dramatic climax of the scene was underway. First, the sound of the bathroom door opening, then the sound of footsteps, stumbling and slow, dragged themselves closer. All this with a backing track of Emmanuelle sobbing, "I'm sorry, I'm sorry. I promise you."

Last night, the wind ripped my window off, and half an hour ago I saw it on the floor in the foyer outside the bathroom. I didn't think about the fact that this was impossible. I thought if I didn't put the window back where it belonged, tomorrow when the doves came, it would be another shitshow. I hurried over there. The bathroom door was wide open and the window was still sitting there on the floor. I picked it up, but just as I was about to start walking, a troubling thought occurred to me. I looked at the window, and then back at the empty frame of the bathroom window. I'd been right to be worried. I set the window back down and stared at the empty window frame: Jean must have chosen this spot for a reason! I pulled myself up into the empty window frame. The height was dizzying. The woman who lived in the building across the way was standing in front of her mirror when she turned and looked at me. I quickly ducked back inside.

•

"Come down! Come down!"

I thought I was having a nightmare, but it was real. Not even half an hour had gone by since they left, but Jean and Emmanuelle were back to square one:

"Come down. Come down."

-2-

A long time ago, astronomers predicted there would be huge explosions on the planet Jupiter. Explosions so violent that if one of the meteors it launched were to strike Earth, the word "tomorrow" would be erased forever from the dictionary of mankind, along with the word "forever." That is, if there were any survivors. And now, the terrifying blows that made every atom of Érik François Schmidt's six-story building tremble left no room to doubt that the meteors of Jupiter were raining down right on our heads.

Terrified, I got up and opened the door. Fereydoon's door was wide open, and he was busy chopping a tree stump with an axe. He looked something like a Greek god with his imposing height, toned muscles, and full beard. With each strike of the axe, every inch of the building's wooden scaffolding shuddered. The dust that had settled in centuries past drifted up through the gaps in the wooden floor, hanging in the air. In Fereydoon's wood stove, a few logs were smoldering and giving off smoke. Three sets of eyes were trained on me from within the half-lit room. Prophet's two glistening eyes were easy to distinguish from the rest.

Fereydoon's well-muscled arms whipped up and down. In the particles of dust and smoke, I saw the enraged ghosts of Montesquieu, Danton, Robespierre, and Jean Jaurès, who were fluttering around in the air, furious at this untimely resurrection. Short of breath, I started coughing. When Fereydoon saw me, he turned and apologized. I closed the door behind me and headed over to my kitchen.

The burning sticks of incense, which Prophet's disciples had hung like victory banners over every door, gave off a strong, stifling smell.

No, to destroy Earth, there was no need for an explosion on Jupiter. It was enough for a few people to show up and mistake an attic room's wooden floor for the courtyard of a luxurious villa.

The latest issue of Bénédicte's newsletter on the wall caught my eye: "These days, when my cat is in heat, it's impossible for me to prevent it from leaving my room. I thank our neighbors in advance for their understanding."

Those days, Bénédicte was in heat and it was impossible for her to prevent herself from leaving her room. And of course, this too necessitated the neighbors' understanding.

Ever since Prophet took the trowel out of his disciple Fereydoon's hand and decided to help Bénédicte himself, she was allowed to go into Prophet's room. Personally, I wasn't opposed to this development, even though their relationship meant Bénédicte would wander back and forth between her room and Prophet's a hundred times a night, Jean Jaurès's bed never stopped hitting the wall for a moment, and Bénédicte's cat would cry at my door till morning.

No, I was happy about it. Whatever the case was, they both became less violent, and it brought an end to the racket made by Bénédicte's saw and Prophet's marbles.

I picked up the kettle to fill it as usual, when I sensed somebody slide past me on the left, the side the bathroom was on. I thought Prophet had slipped into my room behind me with the stealth of a shadow. Panicked, I turned around. But there was no one there. No doubt fatigue and chronic insomnia had made me paranoid. I held the kettle under the tap. But as I was looking down, I sensed that there was someone right in front of me. I looked up and petrified, saw an old man in front of me in the bathroom mirror. I dropped the kettle and it clanged on the bathroom floor.

We stared at each other. I didn't recognize him. His hair was all white, his tired eyes sunken in. His nose was crooked and among the deep wrinkles on his forehead, two diagonal lines had appeared right above his eyebrows—two Satanic eyebrows that reminded me of Mephisto.

I touched my face, he touched his. I traced those demonic lines above my eyebrows, he did the same.

I wasn't happy that I'd finally succeeded in seeing my own reflection. If the Theory of Objects was correct and my mirror only reflected inanimate things, then there was no reason to be happy. A vague recollection emerged from behind the foggy layers of my mind: a chair that was right in front of the door, a set of dusty black clothes, the slight tremble of an upper lip, and a hand hidden in a coat pocket.

I opened the kitchen door and made a beeline for my room. Fereydoon's door was still open. The flames had grown larger and the smoke emanating from the wood stove coiled through the door frame and out into the hall. Fereydoon was sitting on the floor and rolling out a ball of dough with the help of a wooden stick. All around the room, bloodshot eyes were staring at the flames.

I went into my room. The chair was still in front of the door and there was a set of dusty black clothes under the legs of the chair, on the floor. The old dove, which had been sitting on the row of dusty books that morning, had now fallen to the ground, its legs sticking up in the air.

I wasn't worried about the mirror anymore. What did it matter if the Theory of Objects was true or not? If my mirror only reflected inanimate objects—and if it meant I was dead, now that it was reflecting me—what difference did it make to me? Did it really change anything?

No, something had definitely changed. I was carrying a head on my body that didn't belong to me. It belonged to an old man I didn't know.

The smoke had made being in my room intolerable. I decided to go back to the kitchen. When I opened my door to go out, Fereydoon was taking a loaf of bread off the fire with a wooden stick. He gave me an idiotic smile when he saw me. I quickly looked down and went on my way. Bénédicte's cat was crouched at the end of the hallway, staring at me. When our eyes met, it hung its head guiltily.

I went into the kitchen. As I was closing the door, Prophet came out of Fereydoon's room and slinked catlike into his own.

In Bénédicte's room, something that sounded like a large ceramic dish fell and shattered.

-3-

I stood in front of the mirror once again. The man in the mirror's upper lip was trembling slightly. Those upward-slanting lines that had appeared on his forehead, like two demonic eyebrows, lent him a diabolical aura. Someone was knocking. I stared at the old man. Suddenly his lips parted and he said something I could barely hear. I listened carefully.

"It's me, Fereydoon."

It was the first time Fereydoon had knocked on my door. I opened it cautiously. He offered me some fresh bread on a tray and said, "Please, help yourself."

I was upset he'd mistaken an attic room for a luxurious villa courtyard and disrupted my sleep with the terrifying sounds of an axe chopping. Particularly because, for quite some time now, he'd been kicking up dust as he built wooden lofts for everyone and their brother, and it was making it hard for me to breathe. I plastered on a fake smile: "Thanks, I have bread. Just bought some."

I was lying. I hadn't been out for a few days and there was nothing in my pantry.

"It's homemade bread, I made it myself."

For the first time, I felt that this polite young man, who was always smiling and friendly, actually had a stony expression on his face. I hesitated. If I said no, I was making enemies for no reason, and if I said yes . . .

"Don't be shy," he said, holding the tray closer.

The smell of fresh bread made my nostrils quiver. I took some.

After I closed the door, I brought a piece of bread up eagerly to my mouth. I heard a voice. I turned around. The old man in the mirror had lifted his diabolical eyebrows: "No!"

Bénédicte's cat was crying at the door. I was used to it doing that. Whenever Bénédicte went to Prophet's room, her cat would come and cry at my door. The way it was crying now was different though. The reverberations of the cries emanating from its throat held an irresistible magnetism in them that coaxed me out of my room. In the hall, I could hear something tapping against the wall. I thought Bénédicte had gone over to Prophet's room again and the tapping was the sound of Jean Jaurès's bed hitting the wall. But it was the strange reverberation of something metal alongside the tapping that piqued my curiosity. When I opened the door, I choked on the piece of bread. At the end of the hall, Prophet and Bénédicte's bodies were tangled up, in absolute silence.

I closed the door. What did I care if they preferred to do it out there?

An invisible force compelled me to open the door again.

The tangle of their bodies and the violent shaking of the ladder behind them were not the delicate curves of a passionate act. They were the sharp, jagged lines of ferocious violence that sent sparks flying in the air.

I craned my neck out again to look. Bénédicte, of whom only a bit of blond hair was visible, was clawing frantically at the air with shaky arms. The metal ladder, which always stood at the end of the hall and had been used by Prophet as his pulpit, was knocked off the wall. As doors opened and stunned faces popped out, Prophet let go of Bénédicte's throat to catch the falling ladder, suspending it between heaven and earth.

Bénédicte, whose face had turned purple, seized the opportunity to flee back to her room. With a black look on his face, Prophet followed right behind Bénédicte and growled under his breath hatefully, "You whore!"

After the surprised faces retreated to their rooms, the hallway lapsed into silence for a while.

The beds in Room 6 and Room 12 were the devil's beds. And now, considering what had happened to the devil in Room 6, I felt as though all my efforts to escape this cycle of death had been in vain, and it was the devil in Room 12's turn to die. As I reflected on the events of the day, I realized there was a singular meaning behind them. "Come down! Come down!" Now that I thought about it, there was a secret message contained in those words. Just as there was in the vicious attack of the doves, the terrifying pounding of the axe, the attempt on the devil in Room 6's life, the smoke suffusing the entire hall, and that piece of bread which was a reminder of the Last Supper.

This was no place to stay anymore. I was changing my clothes when a knock came on the door. I didn't move a muscle. Another knock on the door. I glanced at the kitchen knife on the table. Another knock on the door—this time, harder. For a second I thought maybe it was the super's wife. (They cleaned so infrequently everyone would complain, and then when they did get round to it, they'd bang the broom so hard against the wall it was like they were trying to say, "Look, see! It's not as bad as some people say. We're cleaning!") But then I remembered that they clean in the mornings, not the evenings.

"Who is it?" I asked.

No answer. I picked up the knife. The knocking was getting louder. I put my ear to the door. I was sure it was Bénédicte's cat, the way it was whining. But a cat . . . how was it possible?

When I heard the sound again, I realized the tapping was coming from the bottom of the door. I breathed a sigh of relief—it was the cat, not Prophet. But the thought that a cat could knock was somehow more frightening. Cautiously, I opened the door slightly. I froze. The bag of trash, which was in front of Bénédicte's door a few minutes ago, had been torn open and its contents strewn by my kitchen door like the guts of some creature killed in a hunt. Was Bénédicte taking her heartbreak out on me?

I opened the door a bit wider. Bénédicte's cat was holding an empty can of fruit juice in its teeth and looking at me expectantly from its corner.

I took a look around. Nobody was in the hall. The cat dropped the can and, looking me straight in the eye, meowed at me disapprovingly. Having translated Miss Emmanuelle's cries, I now had to try to decipher this cat's incessant monotone meows, which were infused with a hint of anger.

I was like a horse that had sensed impending disaster. But I neither whinnied nor stomped my hooves. I ran down the stairs in a flash, taking them a few at a time, and rang the bell for the fourth floor.

-4-

When Érik François Schmidt came in, Gabik let me go and ran over to greet him. When he saw Érik François Schmidt wasn't paying him any attention though, he was hurt and started spinning around in circles a few times, having nothing better to do. Then he hopped up on the faded red couch on the right side of the guest room.

Érik François Schmidt pulled a stack of rent bills out of an envelope and started checking them over one by one. I wasn't sure what to do. I should have told him right away I'd paid my rent a few days ago to save him the trouble, but that would be like launching myself off a cliff when I had no idea how high it was, since I'd have to explain right away why I'd come, and that wasn't an easy thing.

I knew Érik François Schmidt's weak spot. Those days, when fundamentalism was being fired out the barrels of guns in Algeria, I saw his rage and frustration over the atrocities happening there. So all I had to say was he'd let a fox into the henhouse by giving the room next door to Prophet. But I also knew it'd be difficult to convince Érik François Schmidt this was true. He'd come to know Iranians well over the years. He knew we couldn't stand the sight of each other. Everyone came to him up in arms about somebody. Kalantar and Seyyed both accused each other of being spies. The way Seyyed saw it, Kalantar had to be a spy because he always left his door open, and because he had no problem traveling back and forth to Iran despite frequenting the opposition group meetings. From Kalantar's perspective, Seyyed had to be a spy because he never worked, but he dressed well and ate out all time, plus he went back to Iran regularly.

As Érik François Schmidt examined the bills, every so often he pulled one out and set it aside. I panicked—these couldn't all be mine, could they? He must have sensed my discomfort and gave me a half-hearted smile: "He hasn't paid his rent in a year!"

"Who?"

"Milosh. I don't know why he doesn't go back. Now that his country's turned into 'heaven!'"

Only a descendant of Voltaire could be a Communist and rent a room to a refugee who'd fled a Communist country, and for rent that was dirt cheap, too. Even Voltaire wouldn't be able to handle someone falling a whole year behind on rent that low. But Érik François Schmidt let it happen! And he held fast to his principles the whole time: he considered the collapse of Communist governments to be a great betrayal, a conspiracy at the hands of the capitalist world.

Seeing Milosh's unpaid stack of bills and hearing Érik François Schmidt's last sentences dealt me a heavy, ill-timed blow.

I thought to myself, "When someone's so committed to Communism they're willing to give Milosh the benefit of the doubt, they'll for sure do the same with Prophet."

I stood up. Still going over the bills, Érik François Schmidt said, "I can't find it. No problem," and started to write out another one.

Stunned, I sat back down. All that effort not to look at his bizarre nose, all that thinking, day and night, to plan an effective revolt had come to nothing. To add insult to injury, I had to pay that month's rent for a second time.

Mathilde couldn't bear the heavy silence that had descended upon the room, "The weather's gotten quite chilly."

In an effort to pull myself out of the depths of the whirlpool I was drowning in, I desperately clung on to this piece of floating driftwood: "Yes, my neighbor started using his wood stove!"

"Why's that?"

"Probably so he doesn't have to pay the electricity."

How ridiculous! I'd clumsily tried to work Prophet into the conversation, but now that it came up organically, I responded like it was my body that had decided to forget everything, not Mathilde's. It felt like it couldn't have been just a few hours ago that smoke filled the hallway and I tasted fresh bread—bread which was now stuck to the roof of my mouth, smelling like the slimy remains of a thousand-year-old rotting carcass. These events were as distant as a memory lost in the cave of remote history.

Érik François Schmidt set the bill down in front of me. Mathilde stood up. "It's dark. Let me turn on the light."

My hands edged toward my coat pockets while I tried to think of a way out, or at least some kind of excuse. Patting my various pockets with quick, nervous movements, I felt the bulge of my checkbook, which, by complete coincidence, happened to be in my breast pocket.

From behind the metal frame of his glasses, Érik François Schmidt's observant gaze held me in its sights. The two fleshy protrusions on his nose were like the barrels of a gun, trained directly on me.

Like a criminal caught red-handed, I resignedly took out my checkbook. Érik François Schmidt adjusted his glasses: "Nine hundred and sixty-nine francs, and thirty-three cents."

I happened to glance at his nose, the two fleshy protrusions of which were now trembling. He sensed my hesitation and his face went red with shame. "This time there's the quarterly building charge."

Mathilde, who had just turned on the light and was about to sit down, stood up: "Would you like me to bring you a pen?"

Gabik, who had been lying on the couch, also sat up. His ears perked up and he stared at me.

Érik François Schmidt's pen was on the table. I wrote the check and headed toward the door. Gabik was sniffing as he walked along behind me.

When I paused at the door to say goodbye, Gabik leapt over and stuck his snout in my behind.

The door closed behind me, and my legs were trembling. I grabbed on to the railing. I had yet to step up the first stair, when the silhouette of a giant eagle appeared on the top step, making my blood run cold. The bells of Saint-Paul Saint-Louis Church rung out with fearsome strikes, one after the other.

I looked up. Prophet was waiting at the top of the stairs!

-5-

When Murnau's Faust told me Seyyed died young, my stomach dropped. It's true his never-ending games gave me a lot of trouble, but ultimately, I'd laid the seeds of my own destruction. More than anything else, my suffering was the result of stupidity. Even though I knew intelligence was a satanic gift, I was always bewitched by intelligent people. And Seyyed was exceptionally clever. When I introduced him to someone, he would try to figure out everything I knew about the person, in a way that was completely imperceptible. Using this trick, which lent him the powers of a skilled psychologist, people often thought he had some kind of sixth sense. Seyyed's biggest mistake was that he hadn't realized my greatest fault: that I too had been granted a satanic gift. Whenever I met anyone, I knew everything they were thinking at a single glance.

I say my greatest fault because this gift not only had zero benefits for me, it made me isolated. As soon as I realized a person's endgame, I got bored of listening and my mind would start to wander.

It was like that with Seyyed too, except that he was a completely made up literary character I had written some years ago. Now that his existence was continuing on independently of me, I was inspired by his skill in playing games, and by his powers of innovation in inventing new schemes, to try giving in to his tricks. I wanted to find out how far a person's ability to deceive you really goes, and how far the strokes of a pen on paper can take you.

It wasn't his games that bothered me. Whenever he lied to conceal his true intentions, I sensed he was moving his knight two by two or three by one again, instead of two by one. That's when I said to myself, let the games begin. Buried within the massive amount of true information I gave him, I'd feed him some nonsense that absolutely wasn't true. We weren't just competing on the chess board; we were doing battle in the arena of life. He moved a piece with a certain intention, and I, pretending I hadn't understood his intent, gave him a gift laced with poison.

Now wasn't the time for regrets, though. Murnau's Faust homed in on something that had been an enigma for me from the beginning.

"What happened between Ra'na and Seyyed on the night of the accident?" I asked.

"Why should I care? All of you tried to manipulate each other!"

He grabbed the pipe from his friend and took a strong puff. "You Iranians have no respect for the first night of the afterlife anymore. Even when you end up in this situation! We ask you one thing and you always go off on these wild tangents." He then turned to his partner and asked, "Did you change your tobacco?"

His partner, who was invisible again, responded from somewhere nearby, "They keep jacking up the prices every day."

"That's karma for you!" He said, throwing the pipe in the direction of his invisible friend. Then he got up and turned to me: "Okay, my good gentleman! Our work here is done. We've determined your crime. If you don't want to confess to it, that's your problem. Your soul has been tainted. In order to cleanse it, you'll be demoted."

When I was a kid I'd heard some stuff from the storytellers about a wretched, forty-breasted dog. As usual, my mind went straight to the worst-case scenario, "Don't tell me . . ."

"No, don't worry. It's evil Shemr who appears in the form of the forty-breasted dog."

How stupid of me! He knew what my thoughts were before I said them, and the whole time, I thought I'd been hiding things from them that might look bad for me. I gave up on the idea of defending myself, and instead thought I might bargain: "You know very well that dogs live in terrible conditions in my country. Plus, the city recently—"

"What are you afraid of? That the city will throw you some poisoned meat? You, who did everything you could to get someone else to kill you? You, who have no courage at all?"

He'd hit a nerve. The struggle between me and the shadow had been dragging on so long, when I was finally free of it, I'd become addicted to the struggle itself. The struggle became my reason for being, my life's meaning. Especially now that I was carrying a head on my shoulders that was no less foreign to me than the shadow had been.

After Prophet's attack on Seyyed, when it became clear my next door neighbor was paranoid, I began, directly or indirectly, to manipulate his mind. I knew he meditated and did ascetic exercises all night, waiting for the voice of the angel Sorush from beyond. So I would tune my voice to an ethereal pitch and recite poems I'd chosen with diabolical precision. First I'd begin with thanks and gratitude to the divine, then I'd move to a kind of rallying cry:

A seeker on the Path
hoped to see
the place where secrets are revealed.
The Hand of the Beyond came
and pushed
the heart of the uninitiated
away.

Then I would set up the philosophical context a little:

I am no lion who can vanquish my enemy;
It's enough for me to vanquish myself.

Then I played some music that seemed fitting. Mostly Pink Floyd. Especially "Dark Side of the Moon." Once I'd really set the stage, I opened the Book of Revelations and began to read:

I know thy works, and thy labor, and thy patience, and how thou canst not bear them which are evil: and thou hast tried them which say they are apostles, and are not, and hast found them liars.

I know thy works, and where thou dwellest, even where Satan's seat is: and thou holdest fast my name, and hast not denied my faith, even in those days wherein Antipas was my faithful martyr, who was slain among you, where Satan dwelleth.

I know thy works, and charity, and service, and faith, and thy patience, and thy works; and the last to be more than the first.

And the fifth angel sounded, and I saw a star fall from heaven unto the earth: and to him was given the key to the bottomless pit. And he opened the bottomless pit; and there arose a smoke out of the pit, as the smoke of a great furnace; and the sun and the air were darkened by reason of the smoke of the pit. And there came out of the smoke locusts upon the earth: and unto them was given power, as the scorpions of the earth have power. And it was commanded them that they should not harm the grass of the earth, neither any green thing, nor any tree; but only those men which have not the seal of God in their foreheads.

And in those days shall men seek death, and shall not find it; and shall desire to die, and death shall flee from them.

And I beheld, and heard an angel flying through the midst of heaven, calling in a loud voice, Woe, woe, woe, to the inhabiters of the earth.

-6-

He wiggles his toes in his beautiful knit socks from Iran and opens the book . . .

. . . Érik François Schmidt gently massaged the two fleshy lumps on his nose. Lumps that had now grown so large they prevented him from seeing me stretched out between the legs of the chairs, unless he craned his neck and tilted his head down. An old pain flared up, and his toes stung. He closed the book. Something was spinning inside his skull like the needle of a compass gone haywire. He suddenly stood up and decided to go pay Seyyed a visit that very evening. When Seyyed had come by in the afternoon, he was able to get Érik François Schmidt to agree to give him Milosh's room, since Milosh had moved back to his country. After my and Prophet's rooms, this was the sixth conquest he'd managed to notch in his belt.

Shortly after Prophet was arrested, Fereydoon was admitted to a psychiatric hospital. He believed Prophet had fed him some kind of transmitter—along with my blood—which made it so could he listen in on all the rooms. Bénédicte's stove had started making a clicking noise recently. Fereydoon grabbed her by the collar a few times and demanded to know who she was transmitting Morse code to. One time he pulled a knife on Seyyed, asking why he was cursing at him. Seyyed was at a loss: "I'm sitting in my room playing my kamancheh. When did I curse at you?"

Fereydoon sang the melody Seyyed had been practicing a few minutes ago and said, "See? Right there! Why do you keep repeating, 'That limp-dick Fereydoon was a hero in the Bastille?'"

After Kalantar's wife left, he quickly found himself a two-bedroom apartment to try to convince her to come home. (She packed her bags the morning after Fereydoon told her, "Sister, these walls are thin. When you moan like that, it makes my whole body tremble!" As she fled down the stairs she yelled, "I can't take this madhouse anymore! Call me when you find a decent place to live.")

Up until yesterday, a pickaxe had been clinking away on the sixth floor for an entire month. Now that Seyyed had commandeered Fereydoon's room on his side on the hall, and my and Prophet's rooms on the other side, he knocked down the walls between them and was galloping ahead at full speed toward realizing his dreams. His calculations had been correct. Érik François Schmidt, who was hard of hearing, didn't hear anything that was happening on the sixth floor. His only heir was a young man who also lived on the fourth floor, across from his father, and he was such an emaciated, anti-social poet type, Seyyed would really have nothing to worry about in the future.

Despite all that, Seyyed—whose dream had been to knock down the walls between all these rooms—was now faced with two fundamental obstacles: on his side of the hall, he'd advanced as far as Room 5, but Room 6, which belonged to Bénédicte, was unconquerable. The second obstacle was even more insurmountable. He'd knocked down the wall between my room and Prophet's, but the wide staircase prevented him from tunneling between my room and my kitchen. He sidestepped the first obstacle —that is, Bénédicte's room—for the time being and continued to advance by acquiring Room 7, which used to be Kalantar's. Until he could find a way to realize his long-held dream, he contented himself with mounting mirrors as big as doors on every wall in the last room. They were all the same size as the mirror he'd always kept in there. Now when he picked up his kamancheh and sat between the facing mirrors, it looked like those interconnected rooms didn't just extend the length of the hallway, they stretched into infinity. Then he'd close his eyes and play that song Fereydoon thought was a satire written to humiliate him. It was actually a march Seyyed had composed to commemorate his recent victories entitled "The Storming of the Bastille."

After Bénédicte's cat died, every day she started adding a new vase to the collection in the hall. Conquest was the name of the game those days on the sixth floor. Seyyed from within, Bénédicte from without. To the extent that now not only were both sides of the hall flanked with flowerpots, they continued down the stairwell to the fifth floor as well. Whispers circulated among the few residents of the sixth floor, "Bénédicte buried her cat in the big pot right outside her door." Now when it got dark, Bénédicte wandered the stairwell like a ghost, looking for her cat with a candle in her hand: "Miku! Where are you, Miku?"

Roots had sprouted from the bottom of the pots and continued their advances in the crevices between the red bricks lining the hallway floor and the worn-out planks of the stairs. The woodwind harmony, which had fallen silent, now gave way to the dry, fragile sound of Bénédicte's plants piercing wood, stone, and cement.

•

As Érik François Schmidt comes in through the door, he loses his balance. He grabs the arm of the chair to keep from falling, but it flips over and he falls flat on the ground. I leap up from my spot between the legs of the chairs and rush to him. His gold-rimmed glasses have fallen off. The light reflecting off the broken lenses mesmerizes me. I turn slightly; in his face there is a deep calm, as if he's been sleeping for a thousand years. Those huge lumps on the side of his nose are no longer weird; they lend him a stately, almost divine and ancient air. Like a piece of bamboo Polynesian tribesmen pierce their noses with to create the aura of a monstrous eagle. The way he's sleeping puts my mind at ease that tomorrow there will be no whipping.

A thin stream of blood flows out of his nose, skirting around the lump on the right, like it's a hill.

I think of a window. Of a girl wearing a white cotton shirt. The girl crouches down to throw a ball into the alley. The ball rolls down the sloped passageway. It rolls away. Sometimes it bumps into the walls on the right, sometimes the walls on the left. The girl follows the ball with her eyes as it zigzags. The alley is empty. In the distance, the ball runs out of steam. It wobbles back and forth a few times next to a garden wall, hits a tree trunk and stops.

I run straight to the bedroom and start jumping up and down on the bed. Mathilde turns her head, "Gabik, close the window, its cold."

As difficult as it is, I manage to close the window. Mathilde gets up. I walk in front of her, toward the body. Stunned, she stops by Érik's head. "Why is he lying here?" and then a moment later forgets what had surprised her. She spots the stream of blood dribbling out of Érik's nose. She gets worried. And then a moment later forgets what had worried her. Once again, it's like she sees him lying there for the first time, and asks herself, "Why is he lying here?" and immediately forgets what she'd asked. She sees the blood again and then the next moment . . .

I return to my spot and stretch out between the legs of the chairs. Tomorrow, I'm going to sleep easy. Tomorrow, when I piss in the hallway, Mathilde will forget. Tomorrow, Mathilde won't remember I did the same thing the day before. Every time she'll think it's the first time. Which is right now. "Right now."

Reza Ghassemi is an Iranian musician, playwright, and novelist. His plays, which won prestigious awards in Iran, were banned after the Islamic Revolution. He has since lived in exile in France, where he has pursued his career as a musician and writer with more freedom. He is the author of three novels, of which *The Spell Chanted by Lambs* (Candle & Fog, 2015) and *Woodwind Harmony in the Nighttime* have been translated into English.

Michelle Quay is a scholar, researcher and translator of Persian literature. She teaches Persian language and literature, in addition to Iranian cinema and culture, at Brown University in Providence, RI. She holds a PhD in medieval Persian literature from the University of Cambridge, where she studied as a Gates Scholar. She is coeditor of *The Routledge Handbook of Persian Literary Translation* (2022), and has collaborated on scholarly translations of medieval Persian rhetoric manuals as a postdoctoral researcher. Meanwhile, her contemporary literary translation work has appeared in *Kenyon Review, Words Without Borders, World Literature Today, Asymptote, Two Lines Press,* and elsewhere. She was the inaugural winner of the Mo Habib Translation Prize for Persian literature in 2023.

Porochista Khakpour is the author of the novels *Sons and Other Flammable Objects, The Last Illusion,* and *Tehrangeles*; the memoir *Sick*; and the essay collection *Brown Album*.